MOTHERS, MIRACLES
AND MISTLETOE

AN ARIZONA SUMMERS MYSTERY BOOK FOUR

SUSAN KEENE

Publishing Coordinator – Sharon Kizziah-Holmes
Cover Design – Jaycee DeLorenzo

Published by Bent Willow Books

ISBN -13: 978-1-956806-11-3

ACKNOWLEDGMENTS

My sincere thanks to my friends Nancy Dailey and Shirley McCann for their help on this book. Without you ladies, the book wouldn't have been out on time.

Shirley, you went above and beyond with all you did. My gratitude is more than words can express.

It always seems impossible until it is done.

Nelson Mandela

The Legend of Moonstone Lake

A young Native American hunted in the Ozarks. He searched far and wide for rabbit, deer, quail, and buffalo to take back to his village for winter food.

He traveled so far, he got turned around and waited for the moon to rise so he could follow it and begin his journey home. As he sat on a high hill overlooking a beautiful valley below, the last rays of the sun fell behind the horizon. He fell asleep.

When he awakened, a beautiful lake filled the valley. It was so large and deep, he could step into its waters from where he sat. Around the edges, he found rare stones. In a dream, Mother Earth told him all of this would happen.

She told him the stones were called Moonstones and were created from moonbeams. The stone, he learned from Mother Earth, meant new beginnings for the one who wore it. She told him he would have new strength and inner growth.

His mind calmed and his spirit soothed. He abounded with energy. Mother Earth said it would protect all who wore it as they chose a new path.

On his way back to his village, he saw an abundance of deer, buffalo, rabbit, quail and somehow knew Moonstone Lake would be stocked with more fish than the people in his small village could ever eat.

When he arrived home, he called the elders together and told them of his adventure, how the lake appeared to him in a dream and was in front of him when he awoke.

He told of the beautiful stone, sometimes with a

rainbow inside, he found on the shores of what he named Moonstone Lake.

The village rejoiced, broke down their teepees, gathered their possessions, children and elders and moved to the wonderful place he described to them.

It was 1858. Since then, the village of less than thirty-five has turned into a city of twenty-four hundred, and it is the number one tourist destination in the state.

If you look hard enough, you, too, might find a Moonstone on the shore of Moonstone Lake.

CHAPTER 1

I've always loved Moonstone Lake. Everywhere I looked, happy people roamed around the Boardwalk or chatted in groups around town. Sundays were my favorite. Our restaurant, Moonstone Lake Café and Sunday Brunch, opened at ten-thirty on Sundays. We began to serve at eleven and closed promptly at two p.m.

Because we are a tourist destination, there is always some sort of activity ending, one beginning or one going on.

Excitement flowed through the air as we prepared for our annual Moonstone Lake Festival of Lights. The town had hosted it since 1998.

I had every intention of spending my Sunday afternoon strolling around with my dog, Nutmeg, to see the progress. The best laid plans.

I heard screams. High pitched, pleading screams

from the direction of the lake. Nutmeg took off in a dead run toward the noise, and I followed.

It had only taken a few seconds for the area around the source of the yells to fill with people and block my view to whatever or whoever needed help.

Nutmeg didn't seem deterred. She barked as she ran in, out and around the crowd to get close to the action. The people let her through. I saw a small child flailing in the water. No one ran to her aid. They stood by the edge of the lake and shouted encouragement to the child.

I pushed my way toward the shoreline as a man tried to hold a stick out far enough for the child to grab hold. She was too young, cold, and heavy from her water-soaked clothes and winter coat to do anything besides try to stay afloat, and she was failing fast.

The man kept holding out the stick, others murmured and muttered while the child got pulled further out into the lake and began to go under.

Nutmeg leapt into the water and swam toward the child. She latched on to the girl's coat near her shoulder and began trying to swim toward the beach with her in tow.

The yelling became more frantic. Nutmeg could make no progress with the child beating her away and thrashing more than before.

I'm not a swimmer, and I knew the water was not especially deep where she and the dog struggled. If the girl could calm down, she would have a better chance of making it to shore.

Nutmeg fought a losing battle. The girl's coat came off. Nutmeg no longer had a hold and the child went under. She came back to the surface spitting and sputtering water and screaming even louder. In her panic she hit Nutmeg, and at one point, the dog went under.

I heard Keith, the chief of police, who happened to be my boyfriend, yell at me from the shore as he jumped in to help.

Nutmeg was exhausted, and I worried whether she would make it back to shore. I grabbed the child by one arm and Keith took hold of the other. She slapped and screamed at us until I let go, and Keith put both of his arms around hers, in a bear hug, so she couldn't move.

Nutmeg paddled her way back to shore and stood dripping and shivering. We'd had freezing temperatures all week. It took us another five minutes to pull the girl completely out of the water and onto dry land.

Officer Randy Malone, Keith's second in command, arrived and wrapped her as best he could in a silver survivor's blanket.

Sirens, from what I hoped was an ambulance, wailed toward us in the background.

A good five minutes later, a frantic woman came through the crowd. Tears streamed down her face and she covered her mouth with her hands when she realized it was her child being attended by EMTs.

I wanted to hear why the child was alone on the shore and why it took someone in her family so long to find her, but I had to move on and attend to my dog.

Nutmeg lay panting in a pool of cold water, shivering in the sub-freezing temperatures. I wanted to get her home and warm as soon as possible.

Randy came over to us and knelt next to my dog. "Is she okay?"

"I'm not sure," I said. "She's breathing heavily and hasn't opened her eyes. I think she is exhausted."

Randy put his hand on my back. "She's young. Let's get her inside. I'll carry her."

"She's eighty pounds, want me to help you with a two-man carry?"

He smiled at me. "No, I'll bring her. You go ahead. Put some towels in the dryer and warm them up. First thing we need to do is get her dry."

I ran ahead to the apartment. In the kitchen sink I ran water until it was warm and put a little in a bowl for her to drink. Randy and I rubbed her down with the warm towels and dried her with a hair dryer. She stopped shivering, drank a little water and fell asleep on the floor at my feet.

Randy shook his head. "I don't know why the child was alone near the lake. It doesn't upset me nearly as much as the fact no one offered to help her. Had it not been for you, Nutmeg and Keith, the girl would be in the morgue right now. What's wrong with people?"

"Don't be too hard on them. I didn't see anyone I recognized. They were all associated with the festival and didn't know anything about the lake or how deep it might be. Some of them have never even seen a lake as big as Moonstone."

"Arizona, you are much too kind. You need to take care of yourself. Your clothes are soaked, and you're beginning to shiver. I'm going to the hospital to see what I can do for Keith. One of us will check in with you later to catch you up on the details."

CHAPTER 2

Too much happened earlier for me to focus on anything but the events in the water. Now I'd had a hot shower, fed myself and the dog and curled up on the couch with a warm blanket.

I'm what is known as a contemplator. I liked to sit alone and go over every minute of an incident and see what I could remember. We all recall more than we think we do. If you see a robbery, the police question you about the person you saw, the car they left in and other details you swear you can't remember.

I'm sure I can bring to mind aspects of an incident later if I let my mind run like a movie projector and watch with detachment. For instance, I saw the man poking the stick out into the water, I hope in order to help the child. Five minutes later I could not have told you much about him.

Four hours later, I can see him in my mind's eye. He stood about five-feet six, a good four inches shorter than me. He didn't have a coat on. He wore denim coveralls and a black and red checkered shirt. His hair looked shaggy and he had a three-day stubble on his face.

This brought to mind the lady I saw. I'm not sure why I noticed her. She stood at the top of the knoll on the sidewalk and watched intently to the happenings at the lake shore. Her skin looked as though it had never been in the sun. She wore a red cape with a hood she held tightly around her. I could tell her hair was red. I didn't see her face but I imagined it lineless and beautiful. She watched with detachment. I don't know why she stuck in my mind. But I could see her image every time I closed my eyes.

I sat up and put both hands to my mouth. The woman in the red cape. I realized I saw through her. I couldn't have, but I did. As she stood on the hill, I not only saw her, but I remember the church behind her. She didn't block any of it out yet she stood directly in front of it.

Maybe the incident at the lake unnerved me more than I thought.

CHAPTER 3

Keith called around seven and asked if I was hungry. The answer was yes. I could always eat. I couldn't invite him to the restaurant because we'd been closed for hours. No way was I going to cook, and I didn't want to go out.

"What did you have in mind?" I asked.

"Randy and Liz are getting Chinese takeout. They asked us to join them at Liz's apartment, but I knew you wouldn't want to because of Nutmeg. They agreed to come to your place. What do you say?"

"I say yes. It doesn't matter what they bring so long as they add Crab Rangoon to it. When will you be here?"

Keith laughed. "Liz and Randy are on their way to pick up the food. I need to go home and take a quick shower. I smell like lake water and I've never really had a chance to get warm. They gave me a set of scrubs at the hospital so I could ditch my wet clothes, but I'm looking forward to a hot shower. I'll be there in about thirty minutes. Don't start without me. I'll be the guy with the beer."

Randy, Liz and I first met in kindergarten. We went our separate ways after high school graduation. Randy went to the Police Academy. I spent a little time at culinary school, but I'd been raised in a restaurant since the age of six. I had the knife skills and cooking knowledge of someone ready to graduate.

I was given an honorary diploma and sent on my way.

Liz Austin went to the Kansas City Art Institute. We all knew she could make a living with her talents but she signed on as a reporter for The Moonstone Lake Reflection so she would have a steady income.

We all settled down in Moonstone Lake and became fast friends again as though we had never been apart.

Keith came to Moonstone Lake two years ago to take over the position of chief of police when our old chief retired.

No way did I believe Keith and I would end up friends. We had a rocky start. Now we dated and shared a kiss now and then. Something kept Keith at arm's length. I would find out what it was, someday.

Maybe he didn't trust me with the facts of his life before the lake. Right now I was satisfied with our relationship as it was. I loved my independence.

Maybe I wasn't ready to share either. Most of the lake's residents knew my background from my mother. It wasn't something I talked about.

A week or two before Memorial Day the population of Moonstone Lake swelled to well over six thousand and stayed high until Labor Day. We towners had the place pretty much to ourselves the entire month of September and October.

The day after Thanksgiving people began to arrive for the Moonstone Lake Festival of Lights. This was our twenty-fifth anniversary. The festival ran from December fifteenth to January first.

Every year the celebration became more elaborate. All the businesses on the Boardwalk, of which I owned one, sponsored the festival, yet everyone in town was involved. Some of the townsfolk and shop owners made more money during the six weeks of the Festival of Lights than they did the rest of the year combined.

CHAPTER 4

By the time the gang showed up with the food, Nutmeg had taken a nap and was her old self. Randy put all the cardboard containers of food on the kitchen table. Keith had beer with him and Liz brought a bottle of Moscato. The entire apartment smelled like a Chinese restaurant.

I opened the cartons while Keith passed out paper plates and napkins. Randy had brought General Chicken, Egg Rolls, Sesame Chicken, Crab Rangoon, Wonton Soup and Shrimp Fried Rice.

"How is the little girl doing after her ordeal at the lake?" I asked no one in particular.

Keith answered. "She'll be fine. I don't think she'll take up swimming as a profession. She was pretty shook up."

Liz poured us a glass of wine. "Her mother is one of the crafters. Thing is, she says she only took her eyes off the child for a moment and she was gone."

Randy chimed in. "Margie Steever is the mother. The girl is five-year-old Skylar. The emergency room doctor wanted to know where they were staying. If they were like some who were camping in the cold or sleeping in their cars, he wanted Skylar to stay at the hospital overnight.

"Mrs. Steever said she and three other ladies were sharing expenses at the Owl's Crest on old Highway 19."

Keith passed me two Rangoon. "I'm going to talk to the mother tomorrow. She didn't need the police around tonight as upset as Skylar was."

"Yes," Randy said. "The mother said they were with three other female crafters and the little girl said more than once Daddy had gone for hamburgers and would be worried about them.

"It was odd how many times Skylar mentioned her daddy. Her mother ignored it completely. She acted like it was four women and three kids. She didn't mention a man with them."

"Why mislead us as to who she is here with? We don't actually care. I want to talk to Margie Steever again because I find it hard to believe the child was only gone a minute. She has Booth 236. It is way up on the hill. It's nowhere near the water. The kid had to be a mile away from there when we found her."

Liz said, "I'm not going to mention it in the paper. Except for a traumatized little girl, it all came out fine.

"However, I want to hear more about the café's cooking contest. It's a first and people are interested. If I can ask you some questions, I will put it on the community happenings page tomorrow."

I didn't say anything until I went to my laptop and came back with my notes. "Lewis, Aunt Sandy and I decided to have a cooking competition. Since it would cost thousands of dollars to fix up a space where eight or nine people could cook at the same time, we decided to have several categories over several nights.

"Say, for instance, on Monday we could have the best main dish. Tuesday, best dessert, Wednesday, best side dish and so on. The cooks will fix their entries in their homes and bring them into the café to be judged.

"There will be a cash prize for each category and a grand prize for *Best in Show*.

"We have the judges picked out. We haven't asked them, but I'm sure they will all agree to help. It'll be held in the overflow dining room at the restaurant."

"I'm excited about it," Liz said.

"Sorry, Liz. You can't enter. You are on the list to be a judge in the dessert category."

Randy said, "I'd be more pumped if it was a fishing competition."

"Or who can eat the most hotdogs," Keith added.

Nutmeg barked. I could only think she wanted in on the conversation.

CHAPTER 5

Every year I thought life would slow down after the squatters left at the end of summer. Mom didn't like for me to call the summer tourists squatters, but it's what they were. Moms and housekeepers showed up first, usually two weeks before Memorial Day.

They stocked their house, RV, cabin or tent for their upcoming vacations. Most didn't leave until Labor Day. Even if Dad had to work, the family stayed at the lake and the wage earner came on weekends.

Next came the pull-behind boats, Sea Doos and the families. Most of the big boats were stored at one of the marinas around the lake during the off season.

For the first week or two, the tourists hogged the tables in restaurants two or three hours at a time while they caught up and visited with friends they hadn't seen for a year.

They didn't seem to notice the other diners standing in line, whether it be in our place or someone else's.

No matter how much we all planned ahead, the grocery stores would inevitably run out of a popular item. Mom would think Dad made the cabin reservations and Dad thought Mom did. Once everyone settled in to small town living again, the fun began.

The first of December, it began again. Two hundred and fifty crafters from all over the nation came to sell their homemade items.

In May every crafter had to send pictures of their wares to the committee. If they were judged handcrafted and well-made, they were admitted to the show. Actually, it wasn't so simple. Some of the crafters and food vendors had been at the festival fifteen or twenty years in a row.

The waiting list to get a space had over a hundred names on it. I overheard one old timer tell another, someone would have to die to lose his spot and make room for another.

Twenty plus food trucks came in for the six-week stint. Moonstone Lake Café and Sunday Brunch didn't advertise during the festival. The natural need for something other than take out and junk food brought people to the restaurant for our delicious home cooking.

This year Mother and her friends had a booth. Unlike the others, as soon as Mom said she wanted a booth for the wooden toys and puzzles she and her friends were going to make, she was in. Being one of Moonstone Lake's oldest and most prominent citizens had its privileges.

Mom had taken off with three of her friends and went on vacation last year. They went to Florida and then drove to Las Vegas in a new Escalade Mom had rented.

There were two things wrong with the trip they took. First, they failed to tell me or their families they were going. Next, three of her friends had no money and Mom took five thousand dollars out of her savings and paid for everyone's entire trip.

What they learned from the trip was they loved to travel together and Mom couldn't foot the bill all the time, thus, the booth at the Festival of Lights.

CHAPTER 6

Nutmeg and I had a routine. Even though the restaurant opened at six a.m. Monday through Saturday, I didn't go to work early. Every morning the dog and I ran a five mile loop around the lake. Once we returned home, I showered, fed Nutmeg, dressed and we headed to work.

I made it by eight most of the time unless I needed to be there for a special occasion.

Nutmeg couldn't go into the dining room or kitchen because of health department rules. She lay under the hostess table in the front lobby. Aunt Sandy had the hostess job, and she loved Nutmeg, so it wasn't a problem.

Keith came in for lunch and I joined him. "How about we go have a look at the festival progress when you are done here?"

"I'd love to. Any word on Skylar Steever?" I

asked.

Benny came with iced tea. Keith thanked him and then said, "No. It's another stop I want to make. And Mary Christianson wants our rent-a-cops to start early this year. She sent a message and I want to talk to her in person. I want to know if there was a particular incident that caused her to ask for them."

"I won't be done until after six. Lewis and I have a meeting about the cooking contest. It won't take long."

He smiled at me. "We don't have to worry about it getting dark. The entire town is lit up like noon on a sunny day.

"I talked to Stewart Mason the other day and he said they added a million lights this year. He laughed when he told me there will not be a dark corner in the entire festival area."

Keith didn't wear a uniform. He had on a freshly laundered long sleeve white shirt with a Moonstone Lake Police emblem on it and the word, Chief, under it and his name tag.

His hair shone blue black in the florescent light. The gray in his sideburns sparkled white. I got lost in his big dark eyes every time I looked at him. Whatever he looked at reflected back in them like light did on the surface of the lake. After two years I still swooned when I saw him.

Before he left, he kissed me lightly on the lips and said, "Dress warm. There's a wind chill off the lake today. The men trying to fasten Santa and his reindeer to a platform in the lake had to postpone the job until the wind dies down. They did get the arch up as you come into town. This is the second time I've seen it, and it's more impressive than the first time."

Lewis and I had to put off our meeting about the cooking contest. His youngest granddaughter had a program at school and he didn't want to miss it. He left a note saying how bad he felt about messing up my schedule.

I wasn't at all worried about the contest. For Lewis, our head chef, and me, it would be managerial. We weren't even on the judge's list. We didn't want our names anywhere except as sponsors.

I went to the front of the café to say hi to Aunt Sandy before I left for the night. She had the task of closing three days a week and I closed four. On the nights I closed, I still went in early to make sure the entire crew showed up for their shifts and there were no emergencies. If push came to shove, Lewis, Barney, our manager, or Mom would do it. Mom was the last choice. She left copious notes about what we do or did wrong and commanded at least three people to help her.

The thing about a restaurant, when it's been in business for over fifty years, is, most of the bugs are ironed out. I think it would run perfectly well without me hovering over it.

Nutmeg didn't really like to wear her coat. She shrugged and fidgeted as I put it on her. "You'll be glad you have this on after about an hour."

I fixed her a scrambled egg with cheese, her favorite.

We met Keith at the hostess podium. He was

deep in conversation with Aunt Sandy. "There she is," she said as I walked up to them. "Are we still on for tomorrow night?"

"Sure we are, me, you and Mom with buttered popcorn and Casablanca on the tube. And I haven't seen Blaze for weeks."

Blaze was a kitten I found in a dumpster with a dead body. I took the poor thing home to my aunt, the cat lover, who agreed to keep him.

"You won't believe how big he is. I didn't think he would fit in with the other cats, but he bulldozed his way between them until they quit making a fuss."

"I've never seen Casablanca," Keith said.

We looked at one another and then to him. What could we say?

CHAPTER 7

We didn't have to look for Mary Christiansen, she floated down the street toward us as we walked up the hill. Mary is a one of a kind. She and her husband, Chris, ran a small grocery in the middle of town for at least forty years.

Chris died two days after he retired. Mary began to organize the first festival and has spearheaded it every year since. When I do the math, I know she must be at least eighty-five. She still looks the same as ever.

Mary looked like pictures I'd seen of Santa's wife, Merry Christmas. She wore long, festive holiday-themed dresses. They hid her feet and it gave the impression she floated above the sidewalk.

I've never seen her struggle to recall a name, forget a meeting or who does what among the crafters. She greeted every one of them by name, knew their spouses and their children.

"You wanted to see me?" Keith said, as we came upon her in the square.

"Yes, about the little girl last night. How did something like that happen? This is her mother's first year. She makes exquisite quilts, sewn by hand. Do we need to be worried about the child?"

"I don't think so. Arizona and I are on our way over to talk to Mrs. Steever and check on Skylar, the little girl."

"I can only think she didn't read the literature I sent her," Mary said. "It clearly states childcare is provided for all children until age twelve. She can leave her at the church with the volunteers as long as she needs to. Maybe she doesn't realize it is free."

Keith bent down, which he had to do because Mary didn't stand taller than four-feet-eleven, and put his hand on her shoulder. "Don't worry, Mary. We'll tell her again. Now, what is this about wanting the extra law enforcement men to start now?"

She looked up at him with sparkling blue eyes. "You are going to think I'm a silly old woman, but something doesn't feel right this year. I can't put my finger on it. It isn't a person I'm thinking about. It's a feeling."

I could tell by the look on Keith's face, he was taking her concern seriously. "I will put three on patrol beginning tomorrow evening. If you can pin down what is bothering you, please let me know. There will be only one overnight. If there is any trouble, I will increase it. When the festival begins and all of the crafters have their wares out in the open, I'll increase it to four overnight.

"Mr. Mason said with the extra lights he's adding this year, there will not be any dark places on the festival grounds."

Mary turned to me. "I hear you are going to have a cooking contest this year, dear. I am so pleased. Tell your lovely mother and aunt I said hello."

She floated away before I had a chance to answer her.

We hadn't walked much farther when Randy came up to us. "Chief, I need a word with you. Sorry Arizona, this won't take long."

The two of them took a few steps away from me. I began to look around. City workers were stringing lights from the tops of utility poles on one side of the street to the top of the poles on the other. The effect was amazing. It would eventually make a tunnel of lights for people to walk through as they strolled down main street and all the way to the Boardwalk some thirty blocks away.

Then I saw her again, the lady in red. She wore the same full-length cape with a hood. I got a better look at her this time, and since I had my camera with me, I snapped several photos.

The cape she wore still covered most of her face, but I had no problem realizing how beautiful she was. The way she held herself, the regal set of her head on her shoulders and her absolutely straight posture. She had to be someone famous who did not want to be recognized. She turned toward me and smiled. I got a good look at her. She looked so familiar. And then she was gone.

I tried hard to remember if I saw anything on the other side of her. She had been too far away for me to distinguish what I saw behind her and what I may have seen through her.

Maybe I had too many things on my mind. I looked around. Everyone had a job. Considering there were at least fifty people hustling and bustling in the immediate area, I guessed no one saw her, or if they did, they didn't pay attention.

I didn't see which direction she walked, she just disappeared. Then she appeared again, three blocks down the street.

This time she stood near a workman as he stretched a string of lights across to a man on the other side of the street. I let out an audible gasp when I realized I could see the man and everything he did through her body.

It was as though she were made of gauze, and I could see her and everything behind her. It couldn't be possible.

Keith and Randy were still deep in conversation. My first instinct was to interrupt them, but my better judgement took over. No one would believe me if I told them I saw a beautiful woman, a woman I could see through.

I patted my camera. I had pictures now.

CHAPTER 8

The talent of the people who came to the festival always amazed me. Gorgeous handmade quilts, candles, wooden toys, stained glass and mini-Christmas trees to name a few.

It reminded me to check on Mother and her friends to see how their booth preparations were going. I knew Mary and the rest of the festival committee would be in a precarious place if Mother's products were not up to par. They wouldn't be able to tell a founding member of the committee who gave so much to the festival she couldn't be in it. They also couldn't let inferior products represent the festival.

We walked to the other side of town in silence. I tried to take in all of the booths, and I assumed Keith did the same.

The longer a craftsman participated in the fair,

the better folks could remember his location. The oldest were most usually near a food truck or the bathrooms.

Margie Steever's booth sat on a knoll about a block off the main aisle. As we walked up, I noticed the exquisite hand stitching on her quilts. Each stitch the same size and tightly placed next to the one in front of it.

I wasn't a craft lover. The only pictures I had in my apartment were the ones Liz Austin had painted for me since she moved into our building. Liz could paint as well, or better, than any artist in the show. She said the newspaper kept her too busy to enter the festival.

Margie Steever sat in her tent on a wicker chair in front of a portable heater with a cup of coffee in her hand.

"How's Skylar?" Keith asked as we approached. The little girl was nowhere around.

"She is in the motel with Ruth Connelly's sixteen-year-old daughter. It is much too cold for her out here today." She turned her attention to me. "I didn't get a chance to thank you and your dog for helping Sky yesterday."

"No need for thanks," I said. "We were happy to help."

Nutmeg gave out three soft barks.

Keith took a step closer to the heater and put his hands out to warm them. "This weather won't hold," he said. "We should be back into the high thirties to low forties before we get started next week. It will still be a long six weeks for a child so young."

She looked up at Keith. Her face flushed. "There was no one to leave her with. Her father helped us bring all of our things here, but he couldn't stay."

"It's a shame," I said. "Did you know the festival provides free childcare for the children of crafters? I know everyone who works there. It's a fine group of people, and Skylar would be warm, fed and well taken care of...and safe."

"I'll look into it. I feel safer when Sky is with me. Someone might take her."

Keith and I shared a glance. I told her, "This festival has been going on since 1998 and we haven't lost a child yet."

She looked back down at the heater. "They don't have to worry about Skylar's father." A shiver went through her body like she had a bad chill. "I'd better get back to work," she said. "These quilts won't hang themselves."

I knew she had dismissed us. Keith caught on too. Before we left, he said, "Mrs. Steever, if your husband is giving you trouble, I can protect you and Skylar from him."

I didn't think she would raise her head again, but she did. "It is Miss Steever; the man is my daughter's father but not my husband. Thank you," she said in a whisper.

We wished her a good day, reminded her once again of the free daycare and left.

Keith took my hand. "I hate men who bully women. I'm going to tell all the officers and helpers to keep an eye on Margie and the girl."

CHAPTER 9

Last year I took up photography. I did so mainly to take pictures of the lake. I'd always been intrigued by the reflection of images off the water. I began hanging my pictures around the café, and without meaning to, I had a sideline. People began to buy my photos. It amazed me.

My mind went to the lady in red. I took my phone out of my back pocket and looked at the time. Marvin Granger, the owner of Old Towne Photos, closed his store over an hour ago. I would have to wait until tomorrow morning to take the camera to him and have him print my pictures.

I stopped in my tracks and pulled my camera up to my face so I could see the preview window. There were over two hundred photos I needed to go through, discard or have printed. I thought back to the pictures I had taken since Keith and I left the restaurant.

In my head I quickly went through my list. There were two of Mary Christiansen, four of the Boardwalk lights and three of the lady in red. I thumbed through them. She wasn't there. No matter how many times I looked for her, her image did not show up in my preview window.

Gccz, I couldn't wrap my head around the reason I kept seeing what had to be an apparition. I didn't know my real parents. I wondered if insanity ran in the family.

The first photo I sold I took with a group of pictures that happened to have a body in them. It showed two does and a fawn as they drank by the edge of the lake. The trees behind them were naked of leaves. A dense fog came off the water and gave the photo an eerie effect. It looked more like a pen and ink drawing than a picture. But what made it so spectacular was the entire scene perfectly reflected in a mirror image back from the water.

I had never thought of selling it, so when an art dealer from Denver and his family came to Moonstone Lake for a week and he wanted to buy it, I told him a ridiculously high price and he bought it.

Since then, I have become much more proficient with my camera, and hardly a week went by I didn't sell a photograph. The gentleman from Denver had been back once to buy several for his gallery.

Mary Christianson and the committee asked if I would take the official pictures for the festival this year. They usually hired a professional but the costs were getting out of hand. Of course, Randy, Liz,

Keith and Aunt Sandy reminded me daily, I was a professional.

The difference being, I would never charge the town for my photos. The cheaper the expenses for the fair, the more we could do for the town. Every penny went to charities or city improvements. We made enough one year to invest in a municipal swimming pool.

Part of every year's proceeds since have gone to pay the lifeguards and for pool maintenance.

Last year the money went to insulate homes and pay utilities for the townspeople who couldn't afford their winter utility bills. The money also funded an after-school program for the children of parents who worked late or in the evening. It also paid for the free child care the crafters were enjoying while working their booths.

Of course, I said I would be happy to take the pictures. I spent too much time at the café which could run perfectly fine without me.

I owned the oldest family-run restaurant in the state. Fifty years of experience from the relatives before me had it running like a well-oiled machine. I still put in a good fifty hours a week, down from my usual sixty plus. I took pride in being the fifth generation to keep the business going. Photography would always stay a hobby for me.

My habit was to carry my camera on a strap over my shoulder in case I saw something I needed to photograph.

As if by command, I looked up and the lady in red stood across the square from us. Three times in one day, I couldn't believe it. She had her arms crossed and looked my way. I swung my camera around to my hand and took her picture. "Keith, have you seen that woman before?"

His eyes followed the path of my camera. "What woman?" he asked.

I had to smile. There were at least twenty women on the square. I nodded my head toward the woman in question. "Her," I said as I focused on her. "The lady in the red cape." I snapped three pictures in rapid succession.

"Sorry, she must be gone already. Everyone I see on the square, I know by name. No lady in a red cape."

Keith shrugged his shoulders and took my hand. "Let's check out the food trucks and see if there is anything new this year."

Junk food is my downfall. I can have anything I want to eat at the restaurant, but we don't have Hostess Twinkies, Ho Ho's, Snickers bars and such. I kept my apartment kitchen stocked from a little store in town called Discount Grocery.

During the Festival, I wondered if they missed my business. I didn't need to go there with the wide variety of junk food available on every corner. Though the festival didn't open for two weeks, most of the trucks were open and selling to the other vendors.

New this year were deep fried Oreos, fried chicken in a waffle cone, fried Snickers, Navajo tacos and fry bread with beef, pinto beans, lettuce, cheese and salsa.

The old standbys I loved were foot-long battered hot dogs on a stick, funnel cakes, cheesecake on a stick and apple slices with warm caramel topping. I could never pass up a root beer served to me in a pint jug.

Keith turned to me and rubbed his stomach. "This is all making me hungry. How about we hike over to Hong Kong Inn and eat some Chinese?"

"We had Chinese with Randy and Liz last night. Let's go to the café inside the Sunshine Hotel. They have the best hot wings in the area."

He laughed. "Better than yours?"

"Don't tell anyone I said theirs were better."

He and I walked the six blocks to the restaurant with Nutmeg in front of us, apparently knowing our destination.

We paused along the way for me to take photos of the different booths and the fabulous light displays. Every year we held a contest for the best decorated spaces among the craftsmen. It astounded me some of the ideas they came up with.

The Sunshine Pub, as it was called, was packed with people waiting in line to get in. The host told us fifteen minutes to get a table.

Before we could make up our minds if we wanted to wait or not, my aunt Sandy tapped me on the shoulder. "Hi, Sam and I have a table in the back. Want to join us?"

Sam owned the Plot Thickens Bookstore on the Boardwalk. His wife died two years earlier. The three of them had been good friends and Sandy and Sam kept the friendship going.

I looked toward Keith for approval. He grinned and gave Aunt Sandy a hug. "Thanks for saving us. Do you think they will run out of wings before this crowd is satisfied?"

"No, it is like this every Sunday night. A bucket of wings and a pitcher of beer for ten dollars. It's the best bargain in town tonight."

Sam stood to shake hands with Keith and greeted me warmly. He'd owned the bookstore as long as I could remember. Mother called him a saint. He stood about five feet ten, sandy hair mixed with a healthy amount of gray, slight of build and a smile to capture your heart.

Aunt Sandy asked, "Have you been to see Mother and her friends crafts? Johnny Kake is a real artist. The rest make up for lack of talent with hard work. Their toys are amazing. They have cars, trucks, vans, buses, a train, and even a carousel with a removeable horse."

"So you think their booth will be a success?" I asked.

"Yes, my only concern is whether they will have enough product. Six weeks is a lot of time to sell things. I hear you are this year's official photographer."

"Yes, I am. Mary wants me to get a picture of every booth and the people attending to it. It is a vendor gift this year. I haven't taken any yet. People are very protective of their secret displays for the contest."

Keith and Sam began a conversation. It consisted of the St. Louis Hockey Blues and their chances to win the Stanley Cup.

Once the food reached the table, we brought our conversations back together. We jabbered about nothing in particular for a few minutes until Keith's cell phone rang. "Yes, how long ago? Call Jess, an ambulance and the coroner. Randy, tape it off. I can be there in ten minutes. Is Liz there? Okay. Don't let her take any pictures for the newspaper. Actually, keep her out until Jess has everything he needs."

Keith looked our way and shook his head. "Someone broke into the motel room where Margie Steever and three other ladies were staying. One of them shot the intruder. He died before help could get there."

"Can I go along?" I asked.

"Sure, you know the rules. Stay in the background."

"You go ahead," Sandy said. "I'll get a to-go box for your wings. Good luck over there. Be careful."

Keith merely smiled back at her, put his hand on my waist and escorted me out the back door where Nutmeg waited.

We caught a ride on a boat to the other side of the lake and retrieved Keith's SUV. He didn't turn on the siren until we were well out of the crowds still milling around the Boardwalk.

Jess Morgan, the head of the CSI Unit for the area, beat us to the scene. He knelt before a body. It lay immediately inside the motel room door, on his back with its eyes wide open and the blank stare of the dead.

He looked up and nodded to Keith and then me.

"It's one gunshot to the forehead. It's from a high-powered rifle. I was told one of these ladies was the shooter. But I'd say the killer was at least sixty yards away.

"Whoever called this in speculated about what happened here."

"Where did the shots come from?" Keith asked.

"I haven't had time to run any trajectories. But the shot that killed him came from somewhere up high. I'd say maybe one of those trees over behind the parking lot."

Keith shook his head. "I wonder what he was doing here?"

Jess looked up toward Keith. "Exactly what I'm wondering. My biggest question is how did he end up in this room?"

"Does he have an ID on him?"

Jess, who had been kneeling, stood. "I didn't want to turn him over until you got here."

Keith said nothing but nodded his head and turned to Randy. "What did you see when you arrived?"

"Three of the four women were standing outside as were the kids. The fourth woman, a Renee Dover, drove in later. She had three hot pizzas with her from Tony's on Highway 13."

Jess called to them. "Do you want me to turn him over or wait for Chad?"

Chad was Dr. Chad Baker, the coroner for the area. He didn't live in Moonstone Lake like the rest of us. It sometimes took a good thirty minutes for him to arrive.

"Did I hear my name?" Chad said as he came into the room. "Sorry I'm late. Seems everyone is out driving on this cold Sunday night." He looked down at the body. "What have we here?"

No one said anything and Dr. Baker squatted

beside the body. He took a recorder out of his pocket, turned it on and sat it on the floor beside him. "Are you ready, Jess?"

What he meant was, *are you ready to take pictures of everything I talk about in my notes?*

Jess turned on his video camera. It bathed the body in a bright light and Chad began.

"This is Dr. Chad Baker, the scene is being filmed by Jess Morgan. Those present are Chief Keith Wesley, Arizona Summers and the Moonstone Lake search and rescue, and the CSI teams.

"The victim appears to be a well-nourished man in his thirties. There is a gunshot wound to the center of the forehead. We haven't found a slug. It could be in the man's skull.

"I'll know more when I get him to the morgue and do the autopsy.

"The entrance leads me to believe the bullet came from a .243."

The doctor signaled for the CSI men to turn him over. *"The exit wound makes me believe I'm correct."*

Dr. Baker slipped a wallet from the dead man's back pocket and handed it to Keith who read from the driver's license he took out of the plastic protector inside. "This is a commercial driver's license. Jackson Ramp, age 33, white, height six feet two inches. Weight 185 pounds. Brown hair, hazel eyes.

"There is fifty-three dollars in cash, a picture of a woman, and a note with the name, address and room number of this motel.

"Randy, call Marleen Stokes over at Children's

Services in Stanfield. Explain the situation and ask her to send someone for the children. Then let's take the three women to the station and question them away from all this blood.

"On second thought, take the kids to the station, too. We'll interview them first. I'm not sure how long their memories are. Try to keep everyone separated. I don't want them talking to one another until after I have a chance to find out what they saw."

One of the CSI crew, Darrell Young, said, "I found these in his front shirt pocket." He handed the small leather carrier to Jess who handed it off to Keith without taking the time to look at it.

Keith flipped it open. One side held a badge. Keith read the information out loud. "Licensed Private Investigator, Jackson Ramp, member of the International Private Investigator's Union. A non-union trade organization for Private Investigators.

"There are some business cards stuck in behind the credentials. Jackson Ramp 1030 Battery Road, St. Louis, Missouri.

"I wonder which one of these women he was following."

CHAPTER 10

Keith and I sat in an observation room as Randy and Officer Amanda Wade questioned the children one at a time. Randy wore an earpiece so Keith could tell him and ask him things if the need arose. Nutmeg slept at my feet.

They began with Skylar Steever, the little girl from the lake incident the evening before.

Sky's eyes were dry and droopy as if she was too sleepy to keep them open. She rubbed them more than once with the back of her hand. "Hi, Skylar," Amy said, with a big grin on her face, "can you tell me what you remember about the man who came in your hotel room this evening?"

Skylar didn't answer. She stuck her thumb in her mouth, began to suck on it and looked down at the floor.

Randy tried. "Sky, you aren't in any trouble. I

just need to know what you remember about earlier this evening."

"I'm hungry. I didn't get supper," she said in response.

"What do you like?" Amy asked. "I'll get it for you."

"French fries. I like French fries."

Amy and Randy both looked toward the camera near the ceiling. Keith pushed a button on the intercom to the front desk and said, "Get an order of French fries somewhere fast. Take them into Interrogation Room Two. Better get catsup just in case." Keith looked toward Arizona and shook his head. "Want to go home? This could take all night."

"No, I'll stay. I will take this time to let Nutmeg run around outside while we wait for Skylar's food to arrive."

The interview with the child was uneventful and did nothing to shed light on the happenings in the motel room earlier in the evening. The little girl was in the bathtub with her toys and saw and heard nothing.

Amy took her back to the waiting room where her mother waited. Keith still had the women separated so they could not discuss the earlier events with one another.

Anne Connelly was a slight girl of sixteen. She didn't dress in the clothes Arizona saw young girls in around town. Her hair would have hung down her back had it not been put up in a bun. Her dress had little color and hung nearly to the floor. She had the look of a spinster woman, not a young teenager.

She told Amy and Randy she sat on her pallet on

the floor and read a book. She said the man knocked. She wasn't sure who let him in. She heard a gunshot but had no idea where it came from.

The man fell, her mother and her friends huddled together and spoke softly. Minutes later, they called 911. "Are you missing school to help your mother with the other children and the craft booth?"

"Not really," she said. "I'm home schooled and Mom says I am way ahead." She held up a book she had been holding in her hand. "I don't like to read, so other than that, I don't have to do any school work while we are here."

Linda Stern, age fourteen had nothing to add above and beyond what they heard from the Connelly girl.

The officer at the front desk buzzed Keith, and he went to make arrangements for the Division of Family Services to take custody of the kids.

Skylar didn't get her French fries and Keith told the case worker to take the twenty-dollars he had in his hand and drive through McDonald's before she took the children to the emergency shelter.

CHAPTER 11

The night dragged on.

Renee Dover came in the interview room first. She couldn't be described as anything but beautiful. Her long silky auburn hair hung to her waist. She wore tight designer jeans and a tan fitted tee shirt with cap sleeves. Her eyes were vivid green. The thought entered my mind the color might have been enhanced with green contact lenses. She was totally out of place with the other three women who didn't seem to put much effort into their appearances.

"Let's begin with your relationship to the other women in the motel room," Keith said, keeping a tight rein on his tone of voice.

"Margie and I are cousins. The other two women I don't really know. Margie's mom sold her quilts here for fifteen years. She died last year and Margie wanted to try to keep the booth her mom had here and keep selling quilts."

"Sorry about Margie's mom," I said.

"We didn't know if it was against the rules to keep the booth or not, but Margie needed the money and what else would she do with nearly fifty quilts?"

Even with my limited knowledge of sewing, I didn't think anyone could make fifty quilts in a year. "How could anyone make so many quilts in a year? Everything needs to be handcrafted in this festival."

"I'm from San Diego. I flew here to help Margie with the booth. The way I understand it, they have a quilting club with over twenty women. Each woman designs and makes three quilts a year. Margie's mom brought everyone's quilts here and sold them. She always sold out and had orders for dozens more before the show was over.

"After the booth rental and expenses, the women split the money for the sold quilts among themselves."

"That can't be much money between twenty people," I said.

She gave me a condescending look. "I'm guessing you don't know much about quilt making and selling. Each one goes for a minimum of five hundred dollars."

"Let's get back to the matter at hand. Do you know a man by the name of Jackson Ramp?"

"No, is he the man who broke into the motel room while I was out picking up the pizzas?"

"Why do you say *broke in*? The children said the man knocked. They thought it was you coming back with the pizza."

"I don't know who let him in. The door was open and the dead man lay on the floor by the time I arrived with the pizzas."

She smiled sweetly at Keith. "I'm not an investigator, but since he was lying face up with his head away from the door, I'd have to say he came in from the front or had turned to run out the door."

"You say you are from California. Explain to me how you got to Moonstone Lake."

She adjusted herself in the chair and recrossed her legs so the one from the bottom was now on top. She grinned. "I didn't highjack a plane if that's what you mean. I flew from San Diego to Denver, Denver to St. Louis and St. Louis to Stanfield. You people aren't actually in a direct flight path to anywhere.

"Because I know you are going to ask. I spent the night at the Holiday Inn Express in Stanfield, ate dinner at the Longhorn Steakhouse and rented that Toyota outside to get here.

"I don't know this Ramp gentleman, but I don't think he should have been in our motel room.

"So far as I know, none of the other women have a gun, and I certainly don't have one. Is there anything else? Everyone is upset. No one has eaten and the children should be in bed."

I told her. "The children have been put into the care of the state until this is all straightened out. I'm sure they have been fed and are safely in bed by this late hour."

"You took the children?" she said in an unfriendly voice. "They were upset enough, especially Skylar after her unwanted swim in the lake yesterday. I think what you did was uncalled for."

Keith looked at her for a long minute, then he stood. "There is nothing else for now, Miss Dover. The police department has rented two rooms for you ladies at Granny's Bed and Breakfast. After all of your bags were searched, they were moved there. One of my officers will drive you."

She stood, began to say something and apparently decided against it. Before she left the room Keith said, "Please don't leave Moonstone Lake."

She didn't turn around.

CHAPTER 12

Before he called another woman in, Keith turned my way. "Well?"

"I honestly don't know. All you have is a dead man. No sign of a struggle, no gun and apparently bold enough to walk right in the front door.

"Right now my theory is he came in through the front door, realized he was in the wrong room and turned to leave. Someone outside the motel shot him and ran away."

"Well, Detective Summers, it's as good a scenario as anything else right now. I'm going to leave Margie Steever until last. I don't know why. Just a feeling I have." He pushed the button on the intercom and asked Amy to come in. "Amy, take Renee Dover to Granny's Bed and Breakfast. I don't want the ladies talking to one another before I question them. Park your cruiser in the back of the lot near the big oak tree and watch the place until I tell you otherwise. Before you go, I hate to have you wait on me, but could you find it in your heart to bring us each a cup of coffee?"

"Sure." She turned and left.

Ruth Connelly came in the room and stood by the door. In a friendly tone, Keith asked her to take a seat in the chair next to me and across the desk from him.

"Ruth Connelly, is that correct?"

"Yes."

"Where are you from?"

"Granite City, Illinois."

"Why are you in Moonstone Lake?"

"To help Margie Steever with her craft booth."

Keith flipped the page on the yellow legal table he took notes on. "How do you know Margie?"

"We have been friends for years. We even went to grade school together. I also make some of the quilts."

Keith glanced my way before he asked Ruth, "Do you know Renee Dover?"

"I know she's Margie Steever's cousin."

You were in Margie's mother's quilting club?"

"No. I make quilts on my own. Margie told me they were good enough to put in the show with the others, and she would add them if I came to help."

Keith glanced my way. "Mrs. Connelly," I asked, "did you know a man by the name of Jackson Ramp?"

"Is he the dead man from our motel room?"

"Yes, he is. Tell us what you saw and heard."

"The room is small, although we had two rooms

together with the door open between them."

"Adjoining rooms," I said.

She nodded her head. "I was in the second room looking at a magazine when I heard the kids scream there was a man in the room. From what I gather, he knocked once, opened the door, said 'excuse me' and turned to leave. There was a gunshot, and when I walked into the room, he lay on his back with a bullet in his forehead."

"What did you do?"

"I have to admit, I must have been in shock because one of the girls pulled on my dress to get my attention. I ushered the kids into the other room and called 911."

Keith stopped writing notes and tapped his pen on the pad. "Mrs. Dover said she called 911. Are you sure it was you?"

"I think so. I pushed the kids into the room and then went to the phone and called the hotel operator and had her call the police."

Keith seemed deep in thought, so I asked, "Why didn't you use your cell phone?"

"I don't have one."

"How did you get to Moonstone Lake?"

"We drove."

"Who is we?"

"Margie Steever, Skylar, me and my daughter, Anne. We came down in a U-Haul truck."

"So you are telling me, the four of you drove down in the front seat of a truck. Wasn't it uncomfortable?"

"It wasn't too bad. Skylar is little and stayed on my lap most of the time. It gave Anne the middle seat to herself. Margie and I took turns driving. And, we stopped a lot."

Keith tapped his pen on the yellow legal pad he had in front of him. "I thought Mr. Steever came down with Margie and Skylar to help them set things up."

"So far as I know, there is no Mr. Steever. Margie is a single mother. I don't even think she dates."

"Is there anything else you can tell me about tonight? Do you have an angry man in your life? Are you married?"

"Yes, I mean no. I don't know anyone who is angry with me and yes, I'm married."

"Just one more question, Mrs. Connelly. Where is your husband now?"

"He is a long-haul trucker. He drives from St. Louis to Dallas and back every other day. When he is not driving, he goes out with his buddies and they metal detect all over the area.

"As a matter of fact. They would like to come here after the festival and treasure hunt. I doubt they will though. It's a four-hour drive each way and the last thing Chuck wants to do when he is off work is drive.

"We have been married twenty-five years and I've never heard him raise his voice."

Keith told her about the children being with the Division of Family Services, and it brought tears to her eyes. He told her about her room at Granny's Bed and Breakfast and called Randy in to drive her there.

As Randy escorted her to the door, Keith asked,

"Mrs. Connelly, do you own a gun?"
"Chuck has hunting guns at home."

CHAPTER 13

Ashly Stern was up next. She looked grossly overweight. I pegged her at five-feet-four, two hundred pounds and make up to rival Tammy Faye.

Her clothes were fashionable and she wore them well for her size. She also moved like a person of smaller proportion.

Keith pointed to the same chair the other two women had set in. "Sit down, Mrs. Stern. I have some questions I need to asked you."

Nutmeg, who had been resting peacefully for the past hour and a half, raised her head and growled at the woman.

Keith looked at me and then the dog. We had been through enough cases together to know if Nutmeg didn't like a person she had a good reason.

Of course, it didn't mean the lady was a murderer, but something with her wasn't copasetic.

I put my hand down to pet the dog, but she refused to lay back down. She sat up, moved closer to me and didn't take her eyes off of Ashly Stern until the interview was over.

"Well, Mrs. Stern," Keith began. "Sorry to make you wait so long. It's a strange thing happened tonight. A man ends up dead in the rooms of four women and three children. No one sees anything or hears anything."

"I didn't say I didn't hear or see anything, because I did."

Keith and I shared a glance. "What did you see or hear, ma'am?"

"I was in the bathroom of the adjoining room, freshening my make-up, and I heard shouting outside. The room is at the very end of the building. The loud voices came from the side of the motel. It was a man and a woman."

"Let me stop you for a minute. I thought Skylar was in the second bathroom taking a bath."

"Well,' she said, "it just can't be true because I was in there. I am sure Skylar used the bathroom in the first motel room to bathe."

"Could you make out any of the conversation?"

"Why yes." Ashly Stern had a thick southern accent. I wasn't sure how real it was because the more she talked the thicker the accent became. "*A man said, this is not only no place for you, but it isn't any of your business. I told you when all of this started, I would handle it without you and I meant it.*"

She didn't say anything else so Keith asked, "Anything else?"

"No. A woman yelled back at the man. She had a deep voice, but I knew it was a woman. She said, *'I'm the one putting out the money. I want this done my way. Do you hear me? I hired you and I can fire you.'*

"He said, *'Fire me then'*. Next thing I knew, a man came into our room. He looked around, said sorry, and turned to leave. A gun went off and the man fell. I called 911 and the rest you know."

"Mrs. Stern, if you were in the bathroom touching up your makeup, how do you know the man looked around before he opened the door to leave?"

"Oh, I don't know exactly how it happened. Heaven sakes, a man doesn't get shot near me every day. I might be confused."

I asked, "Are you sure you called 911? One of the ladies we interviewed earlier said she called."

Now three women out of the four said they called 911. I knew there was more to this shooting than the women cared to admit. They obviously talked over the incident and who would say what before they called the authorities. They must have not discussed who called the police.

"Well, they must be mistaken." She pulled her cell phone out of her purse and laid it on the desk. "I can prove it. Look at my call log. You will see the 911 call I made on my call log."

"I forgot to ask, Mrs. Stern, where do you live?"

"In Granite City, Illinois. I go to church with Margie Steever, and I was in her mother's quilting club.

"We haven't had a bite to eat since this morning.

Do you think we can be done for the night? Of course, I'm sure the pizza is not any good any longer.

"I must say, it is inconvenient to have someone murdered in your motel room."

I expected her to put her hand to her head and feign fainting. It was a great impression of Scarlett O'Hara.

CHAPTER 14

By the time we got to Margie Steever, I was tired, confused and hungrier than ever.

"Let me get this straight," Keith said. "Renee Dover is your cousin who flew in from California to help you for the next six weeks. Ruth Connelly and Ashly Stern are your friends."

"Yes. We all live within a mile of one another in Granite City, Illinois."

"Tell me what you remember about earlier this evening. Did you know the man in your room?"

"No, I was in the bathroom with Sky while she took a bath. She has been shaky since the accident in the lake so I've been babying her some."

Keith had his pen to paper and was still taking notes, so I asked, "Which bathroom were you in with Skylar?"

"The one in the adjoining room. I remember

because Ashly seemed to be in there forever. I sat on the bed with Skylar and waited for her to come out. She is forever touching up her makeup."

"What did you hear or see?" Keith asked.

"Not much, I'm afraid. I heard a man say, '*oh, I'm sorry*'. There was a pop. It sounded like a firecracker. The other mothers tried to usher the kids into the adjoining room where Sky and I were. I stayed in the bathroom with Skylar and didn't come out until an officer arrived."

"Did you think to call 911?"

"No. My thought was to protect Skylar."

"Did you think Skylar needed protection?"

She put her head in both hands, recovered, brushed the hair from around her face and said, "I didn't until she ended up in the lake."

"Margie, I mean Mrs. Steever, there is much more going on here than everyone is telling us. You need to be honest if you want us to get to the bottom of this. Why would someone want to hurt Skylar?"

"She was with a group of students from her daycare. The teacher decided to take them for a walk. Everyone was told to hold hands and not to let go. They were only going to walk around the block because the sun was shining and the day was warm."

Margie stopped.

"Go ahead. Tell us what happened."

"I'm not quite sure. Mrs. Taylor, the teacher, said a car came speeding around the corner and jumped the curb. The children let go of one another's hands and scattered. Skylar could not be found.

"The school searched for several hours. Finally, the police found her nine blocks from her group, in a park, in the woods, behind a tree, crying.

"She told us a man took her there in his car and let her go. She said the man said, '*I just can't do this. Run little girl. Run as fast as you can. Get away from me'.*

"Skylar hid behind the tree until the officer found her."

Keith looked at me and nodded. I asked, "Why do you think this has anything to do with Skylar wandering off to the lake and the man shot in your motel room?"

"Even though the man didn't hurt Skylar, the police took her to their station and had her look at pictures of men who were likely to hurt children. She picked the man's picture out of a book of mug shots. She put her finger on a picture of Daniel Wade Demount."

Mrs. Steever stopped talking and looked up at us.

"I'm sorry," Keith said. "I have no idea who that is."

"Everyone knows who he is. Daniel Wade Demount, the host of the Wrangler Jim Show. He is on every afternoon at four. All the children watch his program."

"Is there a chance Skylar recognized him from his TV program?" I asked.

Tears formed in her eyes and ran down her cheeks. "I would think so, but Skylar isn't the only child to say he picked her up. There are several others. He swears they all know him from the show. Skylar went to watch it in the studio once with her class. They all love the man. When a class goes to visit, he takes the time to speak to each of the children personally. Some kids don't get special treatment at home. Of course they all remember him.

"All the kids who say he picked them up are not saying it now. Three were boys and their families moved out of state. Of the four girls who say he took them, now they say they identified the wrong man. But he was the only man she recognized of the fifty or so pictures they showed her. She was only five. I have always thought they pushed her toward his picture.

"Every other picture showed men in plain shirts. The picture of Demount was of him in his costume."

Keith leaned forward as if he didn't want to miss a word. "What is his costume?"

"He wears a bright red shirt with beads on the collar and a bright blue cowboy tie, I think it is called a bolo. His cheeks are made up. Each one has a bright pink circle of rouge on it. I think if he was dressed like the other men, none of the children would have picked him.

"I was in there with her. They kept going back to Mr. Demount's picture and asking, 'Are you sure it wasn't this man'? She finally said, 'yes'.

"Skylar is the only one who insists it is him. The other families withdrew their complaints. We are sure they were paid off. A man came to our house and offered us twenty thousand dollars to never mention it again.

"The man said since Daniel didn't do anything to

the children, we should just let it go like the others did.

"Skylar's dad said, *'No way, he would nail the little pervert somehow'*."

"I have two more questions for you Mrs. Steever," Keith said, first, where is your husband now? Secondly do you know the name of the man who came to your house with the offer of money?"

"We are divorced. Tim left before Skylar was a year old. I even took my maiden name back, and changed Sky's to Steever. Tim's last name is Clark. Timothy Robin Clark.

"He stalked Mr. Demount, beat him up twice and said he would not let up until Daniel admitted he took those children. Tim said *'It was just a matter of time before that pervert couldn't keep his emotions in check and a child would end up hurt'.*"

"We have conflicting stories," Keith said. "Skylar says Daddy helped set up the tent and bring the quilts down. Ruth Connelly said she and Anne drove here with you in a U-Haul truck. Skylar said Daddy is out getting hamburgers and she needed to go."

"Skylar loves Tim. He told her he was her daddy a couple of months ago. But Tim had no interest in Sky until this abduction. I know he sees dollar signs.

"Tim is an engineer on Amtrack. He insisted he come down here and check things out before he left on his next trip. He said he wanted to make sure things were safe for Skylar. The train was on secondary tracks in Stanfield. He hitched a ride down and promised her the sky and then left.

"I worry he will cause Demount to do something and Skylar will get hurt."

"I'm sorry to keep you here, Margie, but how long ago did all of this happen?"

"Over a year. Tim won't let it go. Mr. Demount has a protective order against Tim. I am the one who should have a protective order against Demount."

"And the man who brought you the offer of cash for forgetting the entire incident, do you remember his name?"

"It was Jackson Ramp."

CHAPTER 15

Keith took me and Nutmeg home when he escorted Margie Steever to Granny's Bed and Breakfast. He told her not to go further than her booth, he wanted to talk to her again tomorrow.

"Want to eat something before you go home?" I asked him, as we reached the security door to my apartment.

"No. I'm too tired to eat. I couldn't even interrogate Mrs. Steever any longer. I want to put all my facts in order before I speak to those ladies again.

"I received a text from Jess earlier. He relayed a message from the coroner that with the petechiae in Ramp's eyes and the pallor of his skin, he believes the man was poisoned before someone shot him.

"I want to see the toxicology report before I go any further into the investigation. I also want to hear the 911 call for myself. I think I would recognize the voice of the caller." He put his arms around me.

As I moved toward him, I said, "The plot thickens."

Anything else I might have wanted to say got lost in our kisses.

CHAPTER 16

There was a note on my door from my aunt Sandy. She was my mom's sister but Mom was so much older, she was more like a mother to both of us. Over the years Sandy had become my best friend.

Don't care how late you get in. Knock on my door. I looked at my phone. Although it felt like midnight, it was only nine-thirty.

"Hi," she said, as she opened the door before I even had a chance to knock. "How are you?"

"Tired, weary, confused, hungry and wide awake."

"Come in and I'll feed you while you catch me up on what went on at the motel tonight."

"Remember the little girl who fell in the lake the other night?"

Sandy shook her head yes.

"Well, she and her mom are staying with three

other women and two more children in adjoining rooms on Hwy 19 at the Owl's Crest. A man was killed in their room; shot to death, but now maybe also poisoned.

"A private investigator. Every one of them told a different story about where they were when they heard the shot. Three out of the four said they were the one to call 911.

"Nutmeg didn't like one of the women. I'm not sure what it means, but I'll keep it in my mind."

Sandy ushered me into the kitchen. "Sorry you didn't get to stay and eat with us. Will Russell sat at the bar and sang for the crowd. He is so good. I heard him say he would be in Vegas for the next six months."

I laughed. "I remember in high school we would all hang out in his garage and listen while he put on concerts with original songs and music he wrote. I bet his mother feels silly now for coming out every fifteen minutes to tell him to hold down the noise."

Sandy said, "Noise has made him a millionaire many times over. I heard on the street he is going to be here on Christmas Eve to do a benefit concert for the Jacob family. They lost two of their kids and everything they owned when their house burned."

The entire time we talked, Aunt Sandy's three cats, Wynkin, Blynkin and Nod rubbed against Nutmeg encouraging her to lie down so they could climb on her. She was having no part of it. She had her eye on the fourth cat, Blaze.

Nutmeg and I found him in a dumpster during an investigation last year. He went from a scraggly underfed kitten to a big beautiful orange and white tomcat.

Blaze wove around and through Nutmeg's legs rubbing on her, while the dog watched patiently. She finally plopped down and all four cats jumped on her and began kneading her fur.

Aunt Sandy opened the refrigerator door.

"So, what's in there for me to eat?" I asked.

She shook her head at me and smiled. "You are so spoiled. Lewis made you shrimp scampi before he left. He didn't want you upset because he missed his meeting with you about the cooking contest. Do you have a name for it yet?"

I took the scampi out of her fridge and put it in the microwave to warm it up. "What's wrong with *Cooking Contest*?

"There is something else I'd like to talk to you about," I said.

"Sounds serious."

"It isn't really, just something bugging me."

"Sit, eat, and tell me about it."

"You might think I'm silly but there is a woman. I see her all over town. She wears a red cloak with a hood she keeps pulled close to her face. She is shorter than me, slight of build with gorgeous skin and red hair. Have you seen her? I haven't met her, but she is so familiar.

"Don't laugh, but I think she is watching me." I might tell her another time about me being able to see through her. Right now I didn't want to share it with anyone. It sounded unreal to me, and I saw it more than once.

She sat in the chair next to me at the table. "Maybe she looks familiar to you because you are describing yourself to me. You are slight of build, have red hair and a flawless complexion."

"This lady is only about five-six, I'm much taller."

"Well, I haven't seen her, but I will be on the lookout. Do you think she has a booth or is a food vendor?"

"No, no I don't. You'd have to see her to understand how amazing she is. She sort of floats. Most likely an optical illusion because I can't see her feet due to the length of the cloak. It covers her feet but doesn't seem to drag on the ground.

"There is one more thing," I said, hoping she didn't laugh at me.

"What's that?"

"Every time I see her, I take her picture or point her out to Keith. He never looks up soon enough to see her and... well, she doesn't show up in my photos."

"Arizona. There is a reasonable explanation for this. I haven't seen her, but I will be looking from now on. Why don't you walk up to her when you see her?"

"Because she is always across the square or on a knoll or moving around a corner."

I had embarrassed myself. I could tell Aunt Sandy thought I made much ado about nothing. She changed the subject. "Emma says you haven't been down to her workshop to see the progress they've made. The toys are exceptional. I think they will do well at the festival. And, it is keeping her out of trouble."

"I will talk to her about it tomorrow evening

when we are all together. You aren't the first person to say how impressive the toys are."

"Oh, I almost forgot. I'll be late in the morning. Emma has an appointment with Roger in Stanfield to get her hair done. She said it was about time she took it up a notch and went to the best."

I had to laugh. My mother's hair had been every color of the rainbow and every primary color. She changes her look nearly daily. If she decides to go to Roger, *the Roger,* it would be a full-time job for someone to take her. "Why do you have to take her? She had the where-with-all to rent a car and drive it a couple of thousand miles. Surely she can make it thirty miles to Stanfield."

"Ary, you're missing the whole point. Remember when we had our eyes opened to how little time we spend with her? We promised we'd do better. I need a couple of things anyway. I thought I would shop while she is in the chair."

"To each his own," I said. "I really need to go home. My mind is going in circles and I need some alone time. I'm sure I'll see you at work, if not, I'll see you at Mom's at seven-thirty."

We hugged and I watched while Nutmeg wiggled herself free from the four sleeping cats on her back. She had way more patience than I did.

CHAPTER 17

I think Nutmeg was as happy to get home as I was. She ate a bowl of food and went to her bed in the corner of the living room. My goal was to sort out everything we'd heard earlier from the women and children at the motel. First, I needed a glass of wine and a HOHO.

I had a stack of poster paper I got from the Dollar Store. I kept it around for occasions such as this when I wanted to sort out what people said and did.

Keith called it my murder board. They did something similar with big cases at the police station.

With my magic marker I made headings— Margie Steever/Skylar. I put them first because even if they didn't kill anyone, I thought, in my heart, the entire situation revolved around them.

Renee Dover, Margie's cousin, absolutely didn't fit into the mold of the other women. Her clothes were expensive, her demeanor spelled money and her hair and makeup probably took hours but were designed to make her look as if she didn't have to do a thing to herself to look like she did.

Ruth and Ann Connelly were likely friends of Margie's, and in spite of the fact I think Ruth lied about where she was and who called 911, I didn't picture her as a killer. A follower, yes. A killer, no.

Ashly Stern was a woman I couldn't picture sitting quietly with a quilt hoop and a needle designing and creating a perfect bed cover. I had her pegged as a follower. She never fit in and came to help rather than be left out. Again, no murderer.

Then we had the villains. I took out another sheet of poster board and labeled it such.

Daniel Wade Demount. How did the host of a children's show get by with abducting children? Or did he? If you believe Margie's story about the police pictures, someone might be setting him up.

If he did actually take the children, I say it doesn't matter if he hurt them or not. He got some kind of gratification from them or he wouldn't do it time and time again.

Google showed picture after picture of him. He looked to be about fifty, slight of build, thinning hair, about five-feet-five. He could have been Pee Wee Herman's brother. I hoped Keith had all the files on the children. Since it was common knowledge, I thought I might talk to Skylar Steever about it.

Jackson Ramp couldn't have been more opposite

of the television personality. He stood six-feet two, had ripped sinewy muscles, a full head of dark curly hair and, of course, a bullet hole in his forehead.

Everyone said the shot came from outside the motel room. The only person who wasn't in the room at the time was Margie's cousin, Renee Dover. When she came in with the pizzas, she didn't look like anyone who'd climbed a tree in the woods and shot someone.

I listed Timothy Clark in the villain column. The entire story Margie told had a touch of deceit in it.

After I pinned the papers on my living room wall, I sat and stared at them. Nothing popped out at me. Who would want this private investigator dead? Not Tim Clark, he wanted the money the man represented. Not the TV star, he employed the man.

Was it one of the women? My eyes began to flutter. Sleep overtook me and I laid down on my bed. Nutmeg jumped up to join me and when I turned on my side, she snuggled with her back facing mine.

My last thought before I fell asleep; the women, the craft booth, and the dead investigator made no sense.

CHAPTER 18

It startled me when I woke up and realized I'd slept in my clothes. Ordinarily I took a hot bath, drank a glass of wine and put on a sleep shirt and shorts before I retired.

I got up earlier than usual so I'd have time to go to Mother's workshop after my morning run.

A basement encompassed the entire underneath of the restaurant and apartment building.

It was sectioned off into storage spaces Mother rented out. We took the office, enlarged it, bought the necessary equipment to furnish a wood shop, heated and air conditioned it and so was born Santa's Helpers.

Although I supervised the construction of the studio, I hadn't had time to check up on the work. Mom could get into more trouble than any unruly third grader if she didn't have enough to do. She'd been relatively quiet and self-satisfied since she became a Santa's Helper. Maybe this is what we needed all along. We all need a purpose and Mom went from restaurant owner to retired woman with no hobbies or outside interests.

I hoped her group of friends would do other shows or put their heads together and come up with another worthwhile project.

After her last escapade of going on an extended vacation without notifying anyone, Aunt Sandy and I realized we didn't spend much time with her. I was the worst offender. Unknown to us, Mom kept a calendar of when we visited and called. I'm ashamed to say in a three month period I had only visited her once and didn't call at all. The second worst offender was her own sister, my aunt Sandy.

The person who spent the most time with her happened to be Lewis, our chef. He'd been our chef for years. He apparently dropped by on a regular basis to chat with her.

It wasn't as if we had to get in the car and drive anywhere. The four-plex where we lived had a door to the café. Aunt Sandy and I lived on the top floor. Liz Austin and Mom lived on the first floor.

This woman adopted me, educated me, left me a successful and thriving business and I ignored her. In my defense, I didn't do it to be mean. Keith, the restaurant, and my photography took up all my time.

I read somewhere we all have the same amount of time; twenty-four hours in a day. It is up to us how we spend it. I chose badly and Mother's feelings were hurt.

Life is a two way street. Mother didn't consult us when she decided to run a gambling ring in her apartment. She had a Texas Hold 'Em game going all day and night for months until she got raided and ended up in jail.

To make things worse, she had Lewis make food for her, and she sold it to the players which put the restaurant in jeopardy.

On my sixth birthday, Emma Summers showed up at the home I lived in in Phoenix, Arizona and brought me to Moonstone Lake to live. It was twenty-seven years ago and she had yet to discuss with me where I came from, who my family was and how she knew to fly across country to get me. Why me?

Aunt Sandy and I made sure we had breakfast or lunch with her a couple of times a week and I called her more often.

"Well, Arizona," she said, as I walked in, "'bout time you came by to visit. Unfortunately I don't have time to show you around. Margie and Johnnie will be here in a few minutes. They will show you everything. I am going to get my hair styled by *the* Roger."

"What will Wanda think? Hasn't she done your hair for thirty years?"

"She won't care. She told me last time I was in she was running out of ideas."

I turned in a circle to take everything in. There were shelf after shelf of hand-painted toy cars, trains, airplanes, bears, cats and everything under the sun a child might want. They were all beautiful. Boxes of finished product sat in the corner to take to their booth.

"Mother, this is great. I bet you sell all of it. I think you and your friends have missed their calling."

"Glad you like our work, dear. By the way, I asked your Aunt Sandra not to come tonight. There is something you and I need to talk about and it can't wait."

I'd never seen the look on her face she had now. Concern, worry, and fear clouded her features. Her voice dropped an octave. I'd never seen her so subdued.

"I need you to come at six."

"Should I bring anything?" I asked.

"No dear, only an open mind." She walked over to me and hugged me. I didn't think she would let go. Emma Summers was not an affectionate person. A horrible feeling of dread began in the pit of my stomach and climbed up and into my throat. I needed to leave before I threw up right there and then.

In all the years I'd been her daughter, she had never said she needed to speak to me alone. Not even when I took the car without permission, drank beer at the pier with Jess, Randy and Liz and let the car roll into the lake.

CHAPTER 19

The murder happened on Sunday evening. I spent most of the night with my charts. My brain still spun with possible suspects. I added my mother to the subjects occupying my mind.

I needed to get the schedule for the employees done. It worked best if I made it three weeks in advance so everyone knew when to be in.

We had twelve servers, two assistant managers, one general manager and me. Lewis handled the seven line cooks, four dish washers and two sous chefs.

Benny, the manager, took care of the cleaning crew, dishwashers, and bus crew. It all worked like a well-oiled machine until days like today when I didn't have the schedule ready.

I grabbed a coffee carafe, cream, sugar, and a cup. I put it on a tray and headed for my booth in the back corner of the main dining room.

From there I could see the entire establishment and yet stay out of the way of the work going on around me. Everyone knew better than to sit in the booth I called mine.

With the laptop on the table and my excel program pulled up, I could usually make short work of the task at hand. I'd pressed print and in the back of the café near the rear door, a printer obeyed my command. I was about to go pick up the pages when Keith walked in.

No man should be so good looking, nice and loving at the same time. It made it almost impossible to stay on task when he was around me.

He walked up to the booth. "Gotta a minute?"

I pointed to the computer. "I will have if you give me ten minutes. Have a cup of coffee. I'll send someone over to take your order. Eating should keep you busy until I finish this."

"Okay. Are you hungry?"

"While you are ordering, have them bring me an order of French toast with strawberries."

"Will do," he said.

Lewis was at his desk when I walked back to get my schedules. "Hi, do you have time to work on the contest this afternoon?" I asked, as I walked by.

"Sure. Sorry about the other night. The grandkids are only young once and I hate to miss their programs."

"No problem," I answered. "See you after the dinner rush. Say about seven-thirty?" As I walked away, I remembered I'd be at my mother's tonight. I would let him know later.

By the time I returned to the table, our food had arrived. "How can you eat so much?" I asked him. In front of him sat a plate of bacon, eggs, sausage, hash browns, a short stack and maple syrup.

"I was too tired to eat last night and too busy to eat early so, I'm starving."

I slid onto the bench across from him. "So what do you know now we didn't know last night?"

He took one of the pictures he had in a folder next to him and slid it across the table to me. "Plenty. For one thing, Timothy Clark is not a nice man. He seems to be quick tempered and doesn't care if it's a man or a woman he takes it out on when he loses control."

I looked at the photo. "Oh my, he's a pretty boy. Too pretty to be called handsome. Look at those eyelashes. I bet he's a real lady killer."

"He's moved up on my suspect list. Seems the police report the day Skylar was found in the park, contradicts the story we heard. It says Demount didn't take the girl. It says— here, I'll let you read it." He took more papers out of the folder and handed them to me.

"It says Demount saw the girl wandering around the studio grounds and stopped to ask her what she was doing. She said she missed her bus. Demount sat her in the shade of a tree in a small park on the grounds while he called the police.

"The girl agrees with what he said happened. Tim showed up and accused the TV personality of taking his child and pressed charges."

Keith looked up at me. "The truth lays somewhere in the middle. If the man is telling the truth about Skylar, it doesn't explain the over two dozen complaints here about children who insist the man got them in his car, drove them around and let them out.

"My buddy in Illinois told me the studio paid the children's parents off to get them to let it go. No one said the man did anything to the children, and a nondisclosure agreement the families signed makes it nearly impossible to get any information.

"Tim Clark wouldn't accept the twenty-thousand dollars the TV studio gave the other parents and sued Demount for twenty-million instead."

I put my hand on his. "It doesn't explain why he would kill Jackson Ramp. There is much more to this than we know. Remember the old adage; *things are rarely as they seem?"*

They ate in silence for a few minutes until Keith said, "It gets better. Renee Dover's husband died two years ago under strange circumstances. She was arrested for his murder and released for lack of evidence.

"Ashley Stern embezzled money from a church where she was secretary. The church wouldn't press charges. They fired her but no jail time.

"And last, but not least, Ruth Armstrong is on parole. Seems she drove while drinking and ran over her neighbor and killed him. Police reports say it is the same neighbor she and her late husband had a property dispute with. The husband died fifteen years ago in Afghanistan."

"She must have been pregnant when he was killed."

"Looks like it," Keith said. "What a group. I can

see why any number of people would want one of those women dead, but Jackson Ramp seems to be squeaky clean. We haven't released his name to the public yet, but I'm on my way to his house now since his wife reported him missing this morning.

"I hate notifying people their loved ones died. Want to ride along?"

"Oh, Keith, I'd love to but I told Lewis I'd meet with him to discuss the cooking contest at seven-thirty and I have an appointment with Mom at the same time. I need to stay here and talk to Lewis."

"I understand," he said. "Call me after your movie."

I didn't tell him there would not be a movie.

CHAPTER 20

I wished I could keep my mind on everything Keith told me. Seems Margie's friends were an unsavory crew, but the rest of the afternoon I had all sorts of thoughts about what Mother could want. I knew the restaurant didn't have any problems. Maybe she had some disease she wanted to tell me about. My imagination went wild all day trying to second guess her.

At the end of my shift, I went past the podium to visit with Aunt Sandy. "Hi. Sorry you are going to miss the movie tonight."

"Me too," she said. "What's up with you two?"

"I have no idea. When she said she needed to visit with me alone tonight, she looked worried and unhappy."

"I wish I knew something, Ary. Her exact words were, '*We will have to postpone our movie tonight.*

Something has come up and I need some time alone with Arizona'."

"That's it? Did you try to find out what it's all about?"

"Sorry, honey. Your mother is not a secretive person. As a matter of fact she most usually gives out too much information. Sometimes I would love to gag her. This seems to be different." She glanced down at her phone. "You'll know in about ninety minutes and I hope I will know shortly after. Looks like a hug is in order." She came around the hostess counter and hugged me. "You'd better go, I have a feeling you don't want to be late."

Nutmeg came out from under the table and we left by the front door. I decided to run in what I had on, a pair of faded Joe jeans and a blue long sleeve knit top. I kept a ski jacket on a hook near the door. I put it on and we left.

At exactly six o'clock, I knocked on Mom's apartment door.

It opened immediately, and I wondered if she stood behind it in anticipation of my visit.

The lady on the other side of the door did not resemble my mother. Mom never went anywhere or let anyone see her unless she had her makeup on, hair combed and flamboyant clothing adorning her body.

This woman's face had no color to it. No eye makeup, blush or lipstick could be seen. She'd scrubbed clean. The hair she seemed so proud of having fixed by *the* Roger in Stanfield was covered with a headscarf, the kind you saw in movies from the forties. She hugged me and then motioned me to a chair.

She didn't say anything to Nutmeg, but she held the door open until the dog came inside.

Mom ushered me to the lounge chair across from the couch and then took a seat herself. "This is difficult for me, Arizona. Since you know nothing about your life before coming to live with me, the news will not hit you as hard as it has me."

I leaned forward in my chair. "Mother, what has happened? You are scaring me."

"Let's have a glass of wine while we talk," she said. "Do you mind getting it, dear?"

Relieved to escape her sad face, I went into the kitchen to fetch the wine. I handed her a glass and sat back down. We both took a sip, and I sat mine on the end table beside me.

"This is a long story, Arizona. You will want to question me as we go. I ask you to wait until I'm done. If all of your questions are not answered by then, I'll answer all I can for you.

"Thirty-three years ago, a young girl had a child. I never met the girl, your mother, but I knew her mother, your grandmother. At one time we were very close.

"My family flew me to New York, some forty years ago so I could learn cooking techniques no one here could teach me. I met a woman. Jo Anna Reed. The six months I studied in New York, I roomed with Jo Anna. We became close.

"Jo Anna, her husband, and parents owned a restaurant in the Catskills, The Summit Café.

"I visited there while I was in New York and met the entire family including her young daughter,

Angela. At the end of my schooling, I came back here. I lost track of Jo Anna, and except for a card at Christmas, we didn't have any contact."

I picked up my wine and took a large gulp. The heat rose in my neck and made my ears burn. My stomach rolled. She had decided to tell me about my family. Why, I didn't know, but my instincts told me it wasn't good.

Mom stopped talking and stood. She went into the kitchen and came back with the wine bottle and a plate of crackers and cheese I hadn't seen earlier. I could tell by its elegance it was something Lewis put together.

She sat the tray on the coffee table between us. "Here dear, eat a little something if you are going to down wine so quickly. Otherwise, it will make you sick."

I nodded and absently reached for a cracker from the tray.

"Now where was I?" I knew she wasn't speaking to me so I sat there and didn't answer.

"Seven years later, Angela was fifteen, she ran off with a man who had wandered into town and swept her off her feet. Nothing or no one could keep Angie from leaving with the man.

"His name was Bruno Markus Sanders, your father. He was twenty-five at the time." She reached into an embroidered bag on the floor and took out two pictures. She handed them to me. One was a child, the other one a man.

"This is your father, Bruno and your mother, Angela."

I could do nothing but stare at the photos.

Mother remained silent and let me take it all in.

The man looked tall, dark hair, two-day beard, bright blue eyes and a build like someone who lifted weights. The girl was about five-feet-seven. I could tell by the height of the restaurant counter she leaned on. Her hair was the same color as mine. She had a slight frame, a winning smile and perfect teeth.

I could only stare at the pictures. All of the questions I'd had up until that moment were lost in the wonder and awe of what I held in my hands. For thirty-three years I wondered who my parents were, and I was finding out. Right now I would not question why.

"The next time Jo Anna and her husband heard anything more about Bruno, it was an article in the paper in New Jersey about an armed robbery. Bruno's picture was plastered all over the news as the man who robbed a service station with his buddies, and three people were killed.

"Once he was convicted and sentenced, Luke Reed, your grandfather, went to the prison and tried to find out where Angela was.

According to Bruno, Angela disappeared during his trial. He never saw her again.

"Bruno told him they had a daughter and if he could find your mother, who he said some awful things about, he wanted to take the child and give her to his parents to be raised right.

"According to Jo Anna, you would have been about three years old then."

I had to escape for a minute. I went into the bathroom and splashed water on my face. I stared at myself in the mirror and then at the pictures of my mom and dad and then at me again.

I saw nothing of my father in me, but I looked like my mom. We had the same hair color, which was unusual in itself, her build, chin, and her eyes with the corners slightly turned down at the inside edge, like an Oriental, were the same as mine.

Mother called. "Arizona, are you alright? We can finish this tomorrow if you are too tired to go on."

"No," I screamed. "I need to hear the end of this," I said in the most normal voice I could muster.

Nutmeg got up from her resting place and walked to the door. A few seconds later someone knocked. I opened it. There stood Benny, our restaurant manager, with a tray of food. He held it out for me to take. "Lewis thought you two might need this."

I took the tray, said thanks and closed the door. I turned to Mom. "So Lewis knows about this?"

"Heavens no, Arizona. If I didn't tell you all these years, why would I confide in Lewis? Besides, if you look you will see there are three sandwiches, three salads, and three desserts. I'm sure he sent it up for the movie, for the three of us."

Suddenly, I wanted to eat. I always ate when I got nervous. I guess this was no exception. Three glasses of wine on an empty stomach took its toll. I took a ham sandwich off the table. Mom stopped her story. She waited patiently until I took a few bites of my sandwich and sat it back on the plate.

"Bruno was sentenced to life in prison with no possibility of parole. Luke and Jo Anna heard from his parents. They were high-priced lawyers from New York City. They were devastated by what their son did, they wanted to raise their granddaughter.

"Back then there was no internet or cell phones. Luke flew to New York and found out all he could about Bruno's parents. They had horrible reputations for being dishonest, and were described as shysters.

"Your grandparents had a good business, but they didn't have the money Bruno's parents, Debra and Michael Sanders did. They were going to track you down if it was the last thing they ever did. Money was no object.

"One night, out of the blue, Angie called her mother. She told her about you and said she needed to protect you from Bruno and his family.

"This is where I come in. Ironically, your grandfather, Luke, was fatally injured in an auto accident. Your grandmother didn't know what to do. For some strange reason she called me and told me the entire sordid story.

She had taken ill for no apparent reason. Maybe it was the stress of Luke's death, Bruno's situation, his parents' unrelenting quest to find you. No one knew why she wasn't getting any better.

"Angie told her mother where she was. Unfortunately, Bruno's family found out, too. She asked me to fly to Arizona and get you and not to tell anyone. It was totally out of character for me, but I said *yes*.

"I flew out the next week, and found you in an out-of-the-way home for children run by the Lutheran Brotherhood and their wives.

"I told the people at the children's home I had come to volunteer and spend time with the children. There were nine of you, five boys and four girls.

"I had the address and directions to the place, and I still could hardly find it. I have no idea how the Sanders found you.

"I met all of the children, but I knew which one was you the instant I saw you. The people who ran the home told me your mother left you and said she was going to a convent.

"She told them she made huge mistakes in her life and she didn't want to make another one by not raising you properly. She signed over her parental rights and said to make sure you were placed with a loving family.

"Your name at the orphanage was, Mary Beth Reed Sanders. After a week of volunteering at the home, they asked if I could drive you into Phoenix for a doctor's exam.

"When I took you back, your grandparents were in the office swearing and yelling. They wanted you and they wanted you right then. I flagged the taxi down as the driver was about to leave. I grabbed you up, carried you to the car and we left."

"You just took me?" I asked.

"I did."

"So then what?"

"I bought two plane tickets to San Francisco. We flew there. I was afraid to buy another plane ticket or rent a car, so I bought one and drove you back here where you have lived ever since.

"You have always wondered why I had no imagination about your name. Well, it wasn't me.

You and I were sitting in a cable car in San Francisco and I, off handedly, said, '*You are a long way from Arizona , young lady*'. You answered, '*I am Arizona*'. You insisted from then on I call you by the name you chose, so I did.

"No one, I mean NO ONE knew where you were. I didn't want to call Jo Anna for fear the phones were tapped. I couldn't write. No one knew my name or where I came from. I'm most likely one of the reasons background checks are required *before* anyone works with children.

"Finally two months later, I drove to Stanfield, used a payphone and told your grandmother what happened. I told her the Sanders were horrible people and I took you.

"She cried and said thanks. Angela called again a few months later but it was the same thing. Your grandmother was afraid to say anything on the phone. She begged Angela to come home, but she wouldn't. She said she was in Mexico at a convent, and content for the first time in her life. She had no idea you weren't at the orphanage where she left you.

"We had no more contact until Jo Anna died. I got a forwarded letter. It said she had two regrets in life. One was never getting to meet you and the second was not trying harder to keep Angela away from Bruno. She could have had him arrested because your mother was only fifteen.

"The letter said she looked for Angela to walk up the driveway every day until she was too ill to look anymore. Your father is still in prison in New Jersey and your paternal grandmother and grandfather didn't stop looking for you until you were twenty-one. They still post a lost person's ad every year on your birthday."

I stood, walked over to her, knelt down and put my head in her lap. "You must have thought I was really something when I was a kid and said you adopted me so I could run the restaurant."

"Arizona, my dear child, I fell in love with you the minute I saw you. You were scared, loving, trusting and you treated me like I'd been your mother forever. You never questioned why I took you from the home. You didn't question anything until you became a teenager.

"I hope you understand now why I didn't tell you all these years. I couldn't take a chance on those horrible Sanders people taking you.

"I'm telling you now because I found out your grandparents, the Sanders, are both dead. Bruno has been in prison for over thirty years.

"It is perfectly safe for you to know who you are. I hope you won't feel the need to tell this story to anyone else and you are satisfied with who you have become."

She ran her fingers through my hair as I sat there. "So you kidnapped me? How did I get a birth certificate?"

"My dear Arizona, it is a story for another day."

CHAPTER 21

I hugged my mother for the longest time before I left her apartment. My mind spun like a whirlybird in a tornado.

As I walked up the stairs to my apartment, I thought about Aunt Sandy asking me to stop and tell her what happened. I hesitated but walked on across the hall to my own place and went in.

Nutmeg didn't leave my side. She knew something was wrong, but she didn't know what. When I plopped down on the couch with a picture of my father in one hand and a child who was my mother in the other hand, Nutmeg jumped up and snuggled against me.

I put both photos on the table and hugged my dog.

No one knew if my mother was dead or alive, my father had a life sentence in a prison somewhere in New Jersey and Emma Summers kidnapped me when I was six.

She asked me to keep it a secret, but honestly, who would believe me anyway?

I stood in front of my murder chart in the living room and tried to focus on it. I needed to face it. Nothing would get done on the investigation tonight.

My cell phone rang. Keith. "Hi."

"Hi, I'd say it was a very long movie, but I stopped by the restaurant earlier and Sandy had let Benny go early and was closing up. She said you and your mom were talking. Is everything okay?"

I took a deep breath. "Everything is fine. She ran the enterprise I now run and she wanted to go over my long range plans. Typical Mom stuff." I glanced up at the murder board I'd created. "Any headway on the murder?"

"No, only tedious work looking into the backgrounds of the people involved. It could be anyone of them. They are not the kind of people you would want to entrust with anything valuable."

I took a deep breath. "Let's tackle it in the morning. Mom wore me out and I drank too much wine. I think there is a hot bath and an early bedtime in my future."

"Want me to come over and scrub your back?"

I smiled in spite of myself. "No, but I'll take a raincheck. Night." I hung up before he had a chance to say anything else. I told myself it was mental exhaustion.

I put my feet up on the couch and let Nutmeg lay between my legs with her head on my belly. The only question in my mind was what happened to Angela Reed Sanders?

My internet search said there were hundreds and hundreds of people with the name. There were equally as many Angela Reeds. I narrowed it down to Arizona. Twenty-one Angela Sanders' lived in Arizona and thirty-eight Angela Reeds.

Truthfully, it is anyone's guess how she ended up in Arizona in the first place. Maybe she didn't. Maybe only I did.

I put the photos of my mom and dad on the kitchen table. Finding my mother was a daunting task and one I wasn't sure I cared to pursue.

She would only be in her late forties. I fell asleep right where I was.

My last thoughts were, is my birthday really April Fool's Day? And I bet somehow Emma Summers legally adopted me.

CHAPTER 22

The night before last I slept in my clothes on my bed, and last night I slept in my clothes on the couch. My goal for tonight included a glass of wine, a hot bath and my bed.

Surprisingly, I didn't feel disjointed by what I learned about my life yesterday. A woman, a friend of my grandmother's, actually risked her freedom to give me a wonderful life.

Instead of feeling unsteady, I had a new outlook on life. My maternal grandmother and Emma Summers cared enough about a little girl they didn't know to save her from who knows what.

Maybe life with my paternal grandparents would not have been bad. I had no way of knowing, but my gut told me I was where I needed to be.

After our run, I took a shower, dressed with care in a pair of charcoal Anne Klein wool slacks, a white long sleeve silk Liz Clayborn blouse and a bright red blazer from Christopher and Banks and black Clark loafers.

Usually I lassoed my unruly red hair in a scrunchie. Today I took the time to French braid it. My look was remarkably different.

I bounded down the stairs, punched the code to enter the café from our building and stepped inside. Aunt Sandy must have the late shift because Alice stood at the podium.

Nutmeg squeezed past her and laid in her usual spot. After a quick trip through the restaurant and the servers' prep area, I poured myself a cup of coffee and headed back to see Lewis.

He looked up when I walked in. "My goodness, Arizona, you look beautiful. Something special going on today?"

My face flushed. I could sense it begin in my neck and work its way up to my cheeks. "No, Lewis, I decided it was time I began to make every day special."

"I try, too."

"I know you do. Speaking of special days, we need to either make the plans for the cooking contest or give up the idea."

Lewis turned back toward his desk and picked up a packet stuffed with papers. "I have it all right here. December 12th Appetizers, 13th Soup, 14th Salad, 15th Main dish casserole, 16th Dessert. On the 17th we will give out the cash awards and trophies.

"Your Aunt Sandy has called every business in town and we have four judges for every night. Your job is to make up the entry forms, pass them out all over town and have those interested bring the entry fee to the café. Go over to Signs Are Us and have posters made and put them up all over town, also.

"We have done almost everything else for you. It is up to you and the crew to decorate the overflow dining room for the contest and to have a place for judges and contestants. Got it?" He laughed and handed me an itemized list of everything I needed to do and the order I needed to do it in.

"Do you know how wonderful you are?" I asked.

"Yes, I do, now get your beautiful self out on the floor and let people see you."

I blushed again, reached over and gave him a peck on the cheek and went on my way.

CHAPTER 23

Two of the waitresses didn't come in to work. Brandi's babysitter had her baby early. Although she had made arrangements for her mother to take over, her mom wouldn't be back from vacation until the next day.

Sally had pink eye. She picked it up from some girl in her sister's Brownie Troop she helped with last week.

I waited tables, poured coffee and talked to everyone I could. The day went well, but we were excessively busy for a weekday. One of the diners told me a big snow would hit us by nightfall. People were out stocking up on supplies and didn't want to take time to cook at home.

During the slow down between lunch and dinner, I went to the kitchen to visit with Lewis. He slid a plate of the special over to me when I sat at the kitchen counter. Country fried steak, mashed potatoes and green beans. I said thanks.

A ruckus in the dining room pulled me back out front. Margie Steever, Ashly Stern, and Renee Dover were at a booth near the front of the room. Each had a menu and they seemed to be discussing options.

Timothy Clark came stumbling in and now practically laid on their table. I didn't have to be a genius to know he was wasted.

I caught part of the conversation but mostly the women were trying to get him to lower his voice. All I could decern were a few words, *your fault, want to see my kid, it's a shame somebody didn't shoot you* and *Ashly, you have no reason to look down your nose at me.*

I looked toward the back and caught Benny's eye. I put my hand to my ear with my thumb and pinky making the symbol for telephone. I hoped he knew I wanted him to call 911 because the confrontation got louder by the minute.

Randy and Amanda were there within minutes and tried to talk Timothy away from his ex-wife's table. They were not having much luck. Randy called to me. "Could we get a cup of coffee here?"

Amanda had convinced the man to sit on a stool at a high top and pulled another stool next to him and sat down. Randy walked around behind the man and stood out of his line of sight with his hands on his hips.

"What's your name, sir?" Amanda asked.

"Why do you care?"

She motioned her arm around the room. Thank

goodness there were only a handful of people in the place. "These fine people would like to eat in peace. Your manner is scaring them." She pushed the cup closer to him. "Please, drink your coffee, then tell me what your beef with these ladies is."

He chuckled and took a drink of the hot liquid. "I'll drink my coffee, but those aren't ladies."

While he sipped his coffee, I took the women's orders for three specials. When I came back with the food, Timothy seemed much calmer. Randy motioned for more coffee.

Timothy had a story to tell and the police officers were listening intently. "Those three over there shot Jackson Ramp. He's been following them around because of the low life TV star he worked for. I call what they were doing, extortion. And murder."

Randy escorted Timothy outside and Amanda followed. I heard him say. "Let's go down to the station where the coffee is hot and strong and we can hear your entire story."

"Miss?" Ary turned around to face the table with the crafters.

"Yes? Can I get you ladies something?"

"No," Renee Dover answered. "I'm confused. I thought you were with the police. Do you work here too?"

I took a step closer to the table. "No. I own this restaurant. I sometimes help the police with investigations."

"Margie told me you helped save Skylar the other night. You just show up everywhere, don't you?"

The tone of voice Renee used sounded more

condescending than friendly. I stood still for a long minute. I took the time to look each of them in the eye. Ashly Stern looked down. "Yes, I guess you could say that. Right now I need to show up somewhere else, if you ladies will excuse me."

I'd been observing people for years. I learned several facts from our little encounter. Obviously, I rubbed Renee Dover the wrong way at the motel or earlier. Ashly Stern couldn't look me in the eye. What did it mean?

Dinner hour rivaled some of our busiest days. By the time we closed, my feet hurt, and the smile I had plastered on my face, fell off.

Aunt Sandy had taken over the hostess duties sometime during the evening. I'd been too busy to notice. I walked up front to see if she had finished with the last customer. She sat on her stool with both shoes off rubbing one of her feet. She looked up when she saw me coming. "My goodness, what a night."

"I know. Busy for a weeknight. Snow forecasts always boost business. I'm even too tired to run tonight." Nutmeg had already climbed out of her bed and sat beside me. "Hey pretty girl," I said, rubbing her head. "Can I let you out on your own tonight?"

She barked twice and ran to the door. I let her out and went back to my conversation with my aunt. "Did you have an altercation with those three women, the crafters? The pretty one asked me if you really owned the restaurant. She has a bee in her bonnet about you, do you know why?"

"No, not really. I guess everyone can't love my

sparkling personality and charming wit." We both laughed.

It took another hour to finish up. Nutmeg hadn't come back. When I opened the door, snow came blowing in. I gauged at least three inches on the ground already and it looked like a blizzard with the blowing snow.

I called and whistled for Nutmeg but she didn't come. Panic rose in my chest and I began to sweat. Aunt Sandy went with me and we set out to find her.

All I could think about was Nutmeg hurt and lying on the cold ground. She'd had enough after her swim in the lake to rescue Skylar. "Let's follow the path Nutmeg and I use when we run at night."

Aunt Sandy turned around and walked backwards a few yards to give her face a break from the frozen moisture pounding on it.

We were past the square and rounding the corner toward the Discount Grocery when I heard Nutmeg. She had something cornered. I jogged on ahead.

About forty-feet in front of me sat Timothy Clark. He had his back against the front wall of the store. Nutmeg barked and growled in the man's face.

"What's going on here?" I asked Timothy.

"Is that your dog?"

"Yes."

"Well get her off of me."

"Stand down, Nutmeg," I said.

Nutmeg took a step backward but when the man tried to get up, she went back to her original position.

"Mr. Clark, don't try to get up. Sit quietly where you are."

He let out a sigh and leaned back against the building. Nutmeg retreated a step.

"What is going on here? What did you do to my dog?"

He raised his voice. "What did I do to your dog? It's more like what she did to me."

"I thought you were at the police station with the officers."

"Well, I'm not. I need to get back to Stanfield. My engine is off track while we build a train to go on to Denver. I'll be AOL in three hours."

"It might be tough to make it back in this weather. It doesn't answer my question as to why my dog has you pinned down."

An officer walked up to us. I knew he was one of the men Mrs. Christiansen asked for to patrol the grounds. "Do you need help here, miss?"

"I'm not sure. I let my dog out for a run and when she didn't come back I began to look for her. I found her here with this gentleman pinned down. You'll have to ask him why."

He grinned. "I'm John Malloy, and I'm going to take a wild guess this dog is the famous Nutmeg."

"Yes, how did you know?"

Aunt Sandy had been standing behind us and said, "Arizona, I wouldn't be surprised if half the country didn't know about Nutmeg."

"I hope you folks are enjoying your little chat. Meanwhile, I'm sitting on the cold, wet ground with this dog in my face," Timothy said.

"Nutmeg." I tapped my leg just above my knee.

"By me. The police are here now."

The dog gave the man one more ferocious growl and came to sit beside me.

John reached down to give the man a hand up. "So, enlighten me. What did you do to make the dog mad?"

"Nothing really. I just don't think she likes me."

Nutmeg pranced over to a car about half a block down and began to bark again. The officer nudged the man to walk toward the car in question. The window on the driver's side was broken, and about then, the keys fell to the ground when Timothy tried to slip them in his pocket.

Officer Malloy keyed the radio on his shoulder and called dispatch. Someone would be with us shortly.

I didn't know who had the late shift, but it didn't surprise me Randy and Amanda drove up. They parked the cruiser in the street with the lights on and flashing. Ten minutes later, they placed Timothy Clark into the back seat of their patrol car and left.

We thanked the officer and headed home.

As usual when Nutmeg received excessive attention, she pranced all the way home.

CHAPTER 24

Sandy, Nutmeg and I walked home quickly and quietly. The blowing snow made conversation impossible without shouting at one another. On the way home we walked with the wind at our backs, which made the journey easier.

Once inside, Aunt Sandy and I slipped out of our shoes. Snow stuck to Nutmeg's paws and the pads of her feet. "Thanks for another great adventure, Ary. I can hardly wait to get upstairs and into a hot bath."

I turned, locked the downstairs door behind me and climbed the stairs to the second floor behind her.

Our apartments were face to face across the hall from one another. She kissed me on the cheek, rubbed Nutmeg's ears and went inside her own apartment. Secretly I was glad. I wanted to go over my two encounters. I know there were things I saw and heard I didn't remember at the moment.

A few minutes of running the evening like the rerun of a movie usually brought interesting forgotten facts to light.

Nutmeg walked straight into the kitchen and stuck a front paw in her drinking water. I started to fuss at her but realized how smart she was to figure out how to quickly remove the ice from the bottom of her feet.

"Follow me," I said. "Hop in the bathtub and I'll run enough warm water to melt the snow off of your feet."

She barked once, ran into the bathroom, jumped into the tub and waited.

I turned on the water and adjusted it to warm and let it run until her paws were covered.

I swear, she had a look of bliss on her face.

Nutmeg jumped out and stood on a towel I'd spread out for her. I dried her feet. When I went into the kitchen, she followed me, ready to eat.

I was still full from the Wednesday night special I'd eaten earlier. I made a cup of raspberry zinger tea and went into the living room where I could see my murder board.

First, I went through the off-handed conversation I had with Renee, Ashly, and Margie. I remembered when I looked each of them in the eyes, Ashly Stern dipped her head and looked down at the table. What didn't she want me to see?

Renee had taken the time to ask Aunt Sandy if I actually owned the café even after I told her I did. Margie stayed quiet. As I recalled, she didn't even order her own dinner. Renee gave me the order for all three of them. She ordered their drinks, too, and they were all different.

Timothy Clark was another story. Nutmeg didn't bother people unless they were up to no good. It was difficult to believe he was about to steal a car.

I wondered how he got from Stanfield to Moonstone Lake. He must not have driven because if he did, he wouldn't have to take someone else's vehicle to get back home.

With a red magic marker I wrote *number one suspect* on my board and put Timothy Clark next to it.

The phone rang. I glanced at the clock on the wall. It was past eleven-thirty. It had to be Keith.

"Hi there," I answered.

"Hi. I heard from Randy, Nutmeg went out crime fighting again tonight. Maybe I should get her a little vest and pin a badge on it."

"I agree, she is one amazing dog. Did Timothy really try to steal a car?"

I heard him take a drink of something. "Sorry, I've been up at the car in question with Jess, and I'm cold inside and out."

"Not a problem, what did you learn?"

"Oh, all kinds of tidbits. First though, we couldn't get any prints off the car. It has snowed at least three more inches since you were there. He broke the window so the inside of the vehicle was so wet we couldn't get anything from there either.

"We found the owner. He said it was his car and he accidently left the keys in the ignition. He didn't go back outside for them because he said he doubted if anyone would take it in this weather."

"I wondered about that myself. Even if he had a car, the roads to Stanfield are winding and ice covered. Even the locals have a hard time navigating them. I bet he wouldn't have gotten a mile out of town," I said.

I called the B&O San Francisco Railroad office in Stanfield. Timothy Clark doesn't work there. He hasn't worked there for four years. Want to know why?" he asked.

"Of course I do."

"Too many run ins with his fellow workers. The straw that broke the camel's back was when he pulled a gun on a switchman. The railroad didn't press charges, but they fired him.

"I'd arrest him for the murder of Jackson Ramp if I could come up with a motive and the weapon used to kill him.

"Meanwhile he is in lockup pending a charge of auto theft. The man whose car it is works in one of the festival food trucks and he doesn't want to cause waves.

"If the man doesn't press charges, I can only hold Clark seventy-two hours. I hope I can shed some light on the Ramp murder before then. This snow isn't helping any."

"You sound tired," I said.

"I am. Cold makes me tired. It wouldn't be too bad if it weren't for the wind off the lake. I'll let you go. If I can, I'll stop by and see you tomorrow. Night, sleep well."

"You too."

CHAPTER 25

The morning sun hit the snow and made it impossible to see anything without sunglasses.

The ground was pristine. No footprints or tire tracks assaulted the landscape. I could have watched it for hours.

There would be no running this morning. The street crews were too busy cleaning the craft and food truck area to concern themselves with the streets and sidewalks.

I knew each shop on the Boardwalk would make sure the walkways up and down the boulevard were clean.

Jason, one of our line cooks, volunteered to clean our walks and parking lot. He had a plow on his jeep. Although he did the sidewalks by hand, he made quick work of our driveway and the Gray Goose's parking lot next door.

I checked the batteries in my camera, put two more lenses in my carry case and headed out with Nutmeg to photograph the grandeur of Moonstone Lake with six inches of new snow on the ground.

After snapping six or seven shots of the restaurant, we headed toward the lake. You could hear a pin drop. The snow acted like a noise barrier.

The few boats moored on the lake were snow covered and the wind had blown the snow so every limb of every tree and all the benches were covered as if it were white shadowing someone put on them for effect.

As we walked, I looked from side to side for the best shots. I found one at the church. The steeple and bell tower were too beautiful to describe.

By eight o'clock, I'd walked most of the festival grounds and I'd snapped hundreds of shots. I didn't have a care in the world when I stepped into the café forty-five minutes later.

CHAPTER 26

Last night was busy because of the snow and today would be light with only a few diners for the same reason.

We fed all of the emergency workers free. I knew they would all be in sometime during the day. Even with them, I doubted we'd have a hundred customers all day.

I gave half the crew the day off. I don't know how fair they thought my methods of choosing who went home were, but I always did it the same way. If a babysitter or baby was involved, they took priority.

Next came workers who had kids at home from school because of a snow day and had no supervision. If I needed to send anyone else, I flipped a coin with them two at a time and the winner left for the day.

When I finished, Benny and I were left to handle the dining room. Lewis had done the same with his crew and cut down to himself, one fry cook, one dishwasher and a bus boy.

Aunt Sandy stayed at the front to greet people, and today she would also seat them. I loved snow days.

Lewis made two lunch specials for your choice of chili or tomato basil soup with a grilled cheese sandwich or old-fashioned beef stew served with warm rolls.

We had a steady stream of diners but we never had more than three tables full at the same time.

I had plenty of time to look over the photos I took earlier in the day. What I saw confused me because I didn't see it at the time I snapped the picture. At the corner of the church, nearly in the shadows was Renee Dover and a man I couldn't recognize.

I remembered her coat, a Pendleton blanket coat in tan with bright yellow, blue and white patterns. I doubted there was another in Moonstone Lake. I highly doubted there was another in the state.

My camera had a viewer but it only showed me a three-inch by four-inch preview. For the umpteenth time I knew I needed a small darkroom in my apartment. I could put it in the other bathroom and never miss the space.

Since I didn't have one, I would have to take the photos I wanted to save over to Old Time Pictures to have them developed.

This time of year, Charlie wasn't too busy so I knew I could get them back by tomorrow. A thought occurred to me. I'd seen an app I could download on my computer and see a larger image.

I looked around the dining room. There were six folks eating. They all had been served and their glasses were full. I walked back to where Benny leaned against the counter in the kitchen eating a bowl of stew. "Will you watch the dining room for a few minutes? I want to run up to my apartment and get my computer. I promise I'll be back in less than five minutes."

"Sure, no problem," he said, and I speed walked to the front of the café. I waved at Aunt Sandy on the way past, but I didn't stop to talk.

I brought my laptop downstairs and put it on the table at my private booth, found the app and downloaded it.

In a matter of minutes I had all the pictures from my camera on my computer and could look at them on the entire fifteen inch screen.

I'd caught more than one picture of Renee and the mystery man. Besides the one by the church, another captured them walking away from me.

My first instinct was to call Keith but I didn't. The police radio Aunt Sandy had on in the front mentioned cars off the road, two injury auto accidents and a boy injured while sledding.

Randy had been in earlier, but no one else from the police department. He didn't have much to say. His coat and hair were wet from the snow, his feet were freezing and his stomach growled.

CHAPTER 27

Late in the afternoon, I saw the man from Signs Are Us in Stanfield come in. He held a tube in his hand and stopped to share its contents with Aunt Sandy. The café didn't have any diners at the moment so I went up to see what he had.

"Arizona, this is Thad Marshall. He has been making the posters and entry forms for the cooking contest. Do you have time to give final approval with me before we order hundreds of them?"

"Sure, I do. Let me go back to the kitchen and grab Lewis. This is his baby, too."

A few minutes later Lewis, Aunt Sandy, me and Thad sat at a six top near the front of the restaurant and looked over Thad's work.

I loved the artwork. Someone had taken a picture of the front the restaurant, and instead of the Moonstone Lake Café and Sunday Brunch painting on the front window, he'd replaced it with First Annual Moonstone Lake Festival of Lights Cooking Contest. He'd included the date and the categories.

The flyers had more information including the amount of the entry fee, the date of each contest and the printed rules. We all loved them.

We decided on two hundred and fifty flyers and fifty posters. Aunt Sandy wrote him a check and we kept his samples for the restaurant. I hadn't been excited about the contest until I had the details in my hands.

As Thad left, Keith came in. He looked tired, wet, and disgruntled. He leaned down and placed a gentle kiss on Aunt Sandy's forehead and a more familiar one on my lips. "Got any food left?" he asked, as he looked around the corner to the dining room.

"Lots," I said, "you can have one of the specials or order from the menu."

"Well, aren't you special?" Aunt Sandy said. "They haven't let anyone order off the menu all day, including me."

We laughed. "She is pulling your leg. Lewis would never say no to her."

Keith and I headed back to my booth, and Sandy gave us a little happy wave as we left.

I told him the specials and he went with beef stew and a grilled cheese sandwich. "What a day," he said, as he pulled off his coat and hung it on a hook at the back of the room. "I don't understand people. There is no way you could get me out on the roads today unless it was an emergency. Yet we pulled a car full of women out of a ditch who were on their way to Stanfield to shop. They said there would be sales today."

His voice had an angry edge to it but I had to laugh. "People from here don't let a little snow stop them, and the crafters are huddled up waiting for it to melt so they can finish setting up for next weekend. You know we're down to thirteen days before we officially begin the festival."

"Oh, I'm aware," he said in a monotone. "My goal is to have this Ramp murder wrapped up before we have another few thousand people roaming the streets, but I don't have a thing. I wouldn't want any of the people I think are involved watching my back. They are a loathsome crew."

"That reminds me." I pulled up the two pictures of Renee Dover and turned the computer to face him.

"Is that Renee?"

"Yes, it is."

"Do you recognize the man?"

"No, I don't, but I think they are a little too close to be only friends."

Keith said nothing else. He sat and stared at the pictures until his food came and then he ate.

When he finished, I cleared his plates off the table and brought him coffee.

"Where is all your help?" he asked.

"I sent them home. Nothing for them to do on a day like today. Benny and I can handle it."

He sat with his back to the dining room and turned around to survey the empty tables. "Good call, Ary.

"A thought occurred to me when I saw the pictures of Renee. All we have is her word as to who she is and why she is here. It was a rooky mistake I made not fingerprinting the entire lot of them when I had them at the station.

"I only have Demount's, Timothy Clark's and Ramp's. Which brings another fact to light. There is no way the network would let Demount keep his television show if all the stories were true. Something is going on, and I wouldn't be surprised if they were not all involved, including Demount.

"I'm going to dig deeper into all of their lives when I get back to the station. The roads are clear, the forecast is for sunny skies and warmer temperatures. I'm going to turn things over to Randy and concentrate on this murder, beginning with Renee Dover."

He sat with me and drank two more cups of coffee. Lewis fixed a box of cookies for him to take back to the station for the rest of his crew. He said thanks, shook Lewis' hand, gave me a peck on the cheek and left. When he reached the door, he turned around and said, "I'll call you later."

CHAPTER 28

What Keith said about Daniel Demount, I had been thinking all along. After Nutmeg and I ran and ate, I sat at my computer and researched the man.

Daniel Wade Demount, age 50, never married, no children. Born and raised in Chicago, degree in communications from Northwestern.

Began hosting the Wrangler Jim Show in 1996. He is the winner of sixteen daytime Emmys.

Criminal history

Daniel Demount has been charged with a dozen cases of child endangerment over the last twenty-five years. He has never been convicted. The network, CDSF has reportedly paid out over twenty-six million dollars in damages to the families and children who have pressed charges.

I sat and stared at the computer screen for several minutes. Why would dozens of children say

Demount took them and then all take a cash settlement?

Timothy Clark said the offer to his family was twenty-thousand dollars, but if you divide twenty-six million dollars into a dozen kids, you come up with settlements of over two million dollars apiece.

Someone didn't have their facts straight. Money drove more people to commit murder than most anything else.

I wondered if I could get the names of the twelve children in question and see what they had to say about Daniel Demount.

My thoughts were interrupted by my phone ringing. The caller ID read, Keith. "Hi, how is your search into the people involved in the case going?"

"That is why I called. Want to come down to the station? Here we have access to the databases you can't reach from your apartment. I have some interesting things to show you." I looked at the clock; ten thirty. "I guess I could. I'm interested but very warm and cozy and settled in for the night."

"I knew you would say that. Look outside. Amanda is sitting at the curb with the motor running and the heater on high."

"Who could say no to that? Tell her to give me five minutes to get dressed."

"Will do. I bought a small portable heater for my office. I put it under the desk. Our feet will stay toasty warm. I'll see you in a few."

I put on a pair of flannel-lined jeans, a long underwear top with a sweater over it and my ski coat. One look in the mirror told me I wouldn't win any beauty contests, but I would be warm. Nutmeg wouldn't put her sweater on and after three attempts, I gave up.

Keith met us at the door and handed me a cup of hot chocolate with a dabble of whipped cream. He bent down and gave Nutmeg a chew bone.

"Where does a police station get whipped cream?" I asked.

"There is a variety of goodies in the refrigerator. I'd say at least three good citizens a day drop something by for us fellas in blue.

"Tammera and Tiffany from the Huga-Muga sent everything we need to have a gourmet cup of hot chocolate anytime we want, including peppermint sticks, marshmallows and whipped cream."

As we talked, we headed toward his office. When we entered, I noticed the temperature rise. His portable heater did the trick.

"Have you found anything out about our little gang of bandits?"

He chuckled. "Actually, I have. To start with, there is no Renee Dover in Los Angeles fitting our Renee's description or within fifteen years of her age." He held up a picture. It looked like he'd printed off of a website. It showed a grave marker with the name Renee Dover. The dates engraved on it were January 5, 1976- December 23, 1999, beloved daughter of Johnathon and Marylou Dover.

"It would make the girl forty-five had she lived. Renee told us she was forty-five and gave her birthdate as January 5, 1976.

"Our Renee Dover is not who she seems. I have yet to find out if she is really related to Margie

Steever, but somehow, I doubt it.

"I haven't had time to look into anyone else. I sent the information I have here, and a picture of Renee, to the FBI. We'll see what they come up with."

I leaned back in my chair. "This kind of fits into my theory they are all in this together. I'm just not sure how. I found out Daniel Demount has been charged at least twelve times with child endangerment. The charges are always dropped and the network has paid out more than twenty-million dollars to keep him out of jail and on the air.

"The question is, why? I watched an episode of his show on YouTube and it is not great acting. Anyone could do it. Why stick with him? He has a hold over them, but I don't know why."

Keith stacked his papers next to his computer. "Didn't Timothy Clark tell us they were offered twenty-thousand to keep quiet? My math isn't very good but if I am figuring right, it would be over two million a kid."

"Exactly," I said. "Here's my idea. We pay a visit to Margie's booth, and the motel if we have to, and get fingerprints, and or, DNA from some of them. I doubt we can get them all at once but I'd like to start with Margie and Renee and Ashly. They are the three I am most leery of."

"Sounds good. What is your schedule like tomorrow?"

It took me a second to go through my week in my mind. "I close. After I check in tomorrow morning, I don't need to be back until three or four."

"How about you?"

"I have to go to court in the morning. It will only take a minute. I need to give a deposition in a hit and run auto accident."

"I have a brilliant idea. Sometimes I amaze myself," I said jokingly.

"What is it, Sherlock?"

"I have to take a picture of each booth and who works in them for the town council. They have to sign a release giving us permission to use the photos for advertising. I'll take a picture of each of the women involved. We will have their fingerprints and handwriting."

"Okay, so it is brilliant. See you in the morning. Amanda is going to take you home. I'm on call so I'm going to sleep here."

CHAPTER 29

No one would ever know about yesterday's snow if it were not for the piles of it at the edges of parking lots around Moonstone Lake.

The sun shined brightly and the temperature had soared to thirty-eight degrees.

The downside to all of this was mud. Mud on the paths, mud all over the festival grounds, people's shoes, our floors and everyone else's.

Everyone came back to work, and everyone in town came out to eat. The restaurant had been a mad house from six in the morning. I decided to go ahead with my plans for taking pictures of those I deemed involved in the murder of Jackson Ramp.

Before we left, I called Pawsitivily Devine Grooming and made an appointment for Nutmeg later in the day. She, above all else, could attract dirt and mud faster than anyone.

Moonstone Lake looked like a wonderland, even in the bright sunshine. Lights were on all day and night. The sun caught the color and it glimmered and shimmered in the light.

I didn't look up much on the way up the hill to Margie Steever's booth. It took all of my attention to avoid the biggest muddy spots.

As I turned the corner at Twelfth and Main, I saw the person I dubbed The Lady in Red. She had her head down as she climbed the hill. For no reason I could phantom, she turned my way and stopped.

I hadn't had this good of a look at her before. She looked between forty and fifty years old. She didn't have hold of the hood on the cape and it gaped open. Her hair and mine were the same color. The difference I could see was she had no curl and gray streaks.

Her hair hung straight down and framed her thin, lovely face. She made no attempt to look away. She blatantly stood and looked straight at me.

I began to walk toward her. When I got within fifty yards, I looked down to make sure I avoided a puddle on the sidewalk. When I looked up, she was no longer there.

Nutmeg and I went to the top of the hill and I looked in every direction. I'd been so mesmerized, I hadn't bothered to take her picture.

I asked two men who were cleaning the walks with scrapers if they had seen a lady in a red cape. Their answer, of course, was no.

It is difficult to put into words the feelings I had when I saw her. I had appendicitis at age ten. When

I woke up after surgery, I had the strangest sensation. Everything in the room glowed an eerie gold.

I heard voices, but a calm covered me with such serenity I didn't want to go back to sleep, but I didn't want to wake up either. This is how I felt when the Lady appeared. I'd give anything to be close to her and share a few words. How silly, I thought. I'm losing my mind.

Skylar Steever's voice brought me out of my stupor. "Hi, Miss Summers. What brings you here?"

"I came to take your picture. I must say I came on the right day. You look beautiful." Skylar blushed and turned the same color as the bright coat she wore. "Is your mom around?"

"She will be right back. She went to the truck over there on the corner to get us lunch. I love hotdogs on a stick and root beer." She held out an apple. "Mom says if I don't eat this this afternoon, my hotdog eating days are over."

I looked toward the food truck to see how many people were in line in front of Margie when I heard a voice I recognized as Renee Dover. "Well, Miss Summers. Aren't you a jack-of-all- trades? Let's see if I can list all your talents. Super sleuth, business owner and now photographer, did I miss anything?"

I knew my blood boiled because it started at my feet and rushed to my head where on its way, I'm sure it made my face scarlet red.

Before I thought of an answer, she added, "I forgot. Dog trainer extraordinaire."

Keith walked up, and the situation defused itself.

"I'll take my leave," she said. "This isn't my

booth, so you don't need my photo."

"Oh, but we do," I said, "it is part of the agreement Margie or her mother signed. We photograph everyone who has anything to do with the festival, and the waiver she signed gives us permission to use your picture for advertising and to award prizes."

"I don't think anyone has a right to give you a waiver for me. Again, you can't have my picture for your advertisements."

Keith, who had been standing next to Skylar stepped forward. "I'm sorry, Miss Dover. It is just a custom we have here. You would be the first one to refuse in the twenty-five years we've put on this event." He smiled his winning smile at her and she took a step backward.

"Well," she said. "If you must, let's get it over with."

I smiled sweetly. "We were hoping to take a photo of everyone at the same time. Are you expecting Ann and Ashly anytime soon?"

Margie Steever must have heard as she walked up. "No, we won't ever all be here together. We have a schedule. There will be two of us on and two of us watching the children."

"I guess we can live with that," I said. "We'll start with you two, and you can tell me when the others will be here."

I snapped several pictures of the two women and a few of Skylar. When I laid out the waivers for the women to sign, Renee spoke up. "I thought you already had a waiver."

"Yes, those are temporary to get the names of

those involved. We get individual ones when crafters arrive."

She looked at Margie who smiled at her and imperceptibly shook her head yes. Renee signed it with a flourish and practically threw it at me. "Is there anything else, Miss Summers?"

"No, and you can call me Arizona or Ary."

"I prefer Miss Summers," she said and turned on her heel to leave the tent.

CHAPTER 30

Keith and I said goodbye and moved on to the next tent to take pictures. I thought it looked more realistic than if we walked off and didn't photograph anyone else's booth.

I knew Mrs. Crammer, the lady in the next booth and her grown son who always took a vacation from his job to help his mom. Georgia Crammer made angels. They were absolutely wonderful.

Some were happy, others stoic, some religious, others whimsical. Over the years, I thought about collecting them.

I didn't have pictures on my walls except for the photos I took. If I had to make a living interior decorating, I would surely starve.

On the way back to the café, we stopped by Mother's booth. She and Johnny Kake, Margie Gold and Riley Durum were all there.

The booth was a child's paradise. They actually had two booths put together. In the far corners there were doors and a table and chair for a worker to sit.

Quite ingenious. In order to leave the area the customer had to exit past one of the owners. I couldn't see anyone stealing from Mother's booth.

The displays were delightful. Near the top of the tent, a platform held one or two of each of their models. One of the trains ran on batteries and clattered around the entire perimeter of the tents.

Each item had a clearly legible price on it, and the bags they had hanging near each pay station were imprinted with *Santa's Helpers* and had a website and phone number listed. Who knew they were even capable of such marketing?

Instantly, I felt ashamed of my thoughts. My mother ran the most successful restaurant in the state for forty years before I took over a few years ago.

After Mother said hello to me, she turned to Keith. "Are you sure you have enough people to keep all of the merchandise at this festival safe?"

"I do, Mrs. Summers. No shoppers or walkers of any kind are allowed inside the perimeter from ten at night until eight in the morning. Everyone has sides and ends for their booths which makes them extremely dark inside. A flashlight is easily visible for blocks around. The men don't sleep when they are on night patrol.

"We supply them with coffee all night and only require four-hour shifts so no one will lie down on the job, so to speak.

"But, you are more than welcome to hire your

own security. We insist whoever you hire come by the station and register, take a short class on how to handle situations they may encounter over six weeks. We also provide a name plaque with the person's name, who they work for, and the word SECURITY on it in bold letters."

"Oh, Chief, I feel so much better. You don't have anyone in mind who would like to work for us in that capacity, do you?"

"As a matter of fact, I have a list of about a dozen men and women who wanted to work this year and didn't get in quick enough to land a job. I can send one of our officers around with the list if you'd like."

"Keith, I would sleep better knowing all of our hard work was in capable hands when we are not here. I don't like to play the *age* card, but none of us involved with this booth are under seventy-eight years old."

"I have one more suggestion for you. The festival committee has rented dozens of golf carts to help our senior crafters navigate the grounds. Sign up quickly before they are all spoken for.

"They are a real luxury after a long day of dealing with people."

"Well, aren't you sweet. I'll do it first thing in the morning."

Johnny Kake said, "I believe I will go over to the festival office now and sign up. These old legs aren't what they used to be."

We said our goodbyes and moved on to an open food truck. "Have you had lunch?" Keith asked.

"No, I haven't as yet had breakfast. And I can

never turn down a pulled pork sandwich topped with coleslaw and a warm cup of Wassail."

Keith ordered and we sat down at one of the many empty tables and ate. Nutmeg had a pork sandwich also, sans the BBQ sauce and slaw.

By three-thirty, I kissed Keith goodbye at the door and checked into work.

He told me he would be at the station the rest of the evening researching. He'd received two texts from the FBI about Renee Dover and another about Ashly Stern.

I could hardly wait to hear what he learned.

CHAPTER 31

Someone knocked on my door about nine. It could only be one of four people. Aunt Sandy, Liz Austin, Mother or Keith. All of them lived in the building except Keith.

He had all the codes due to an emergency we had several years ago where he needed to get into the building and couldn't. I saw no reason to change the codes to keep him out.

My door didn't have a peep hole. I really didn't need one. When I opened it, Keith stepped in.

He had an armload of papers he quickly placed on the couch and took me in his arms. "I love solving crimes with you, but sometimes we get so engrossed in a crime, I get lonesome."

I kissed him and he kissed me back. One thing might have led to another had I not said, "What are you doing here? I thought you were tracking down our suspects' pasts."

"I was, and I did. I didn't want to text you all of this information and well, mostly I wanted to see your face when I tell you what I found out."

"Don't keep me in suspense? Want a beer?"

"No, I'm still on call. I would take a cup of coffee, though. As much as I love hot chocolate, which is the drink of choice at the station right now, it begins to get too sweet for me."

I went to the Keurig and made him a cup. "Do you want to sit at the kitchen table?"

"No, no more stiff, straight-back chairs in my future."

Keith had been ignoring Nutmeg who let him know it by jumping on his lap and licking his face as soon as his butt hit the sofa cushion. "I'm sorry, Miss Nutmeg. Too much on my mind this evening." He patted the space next to him. "Want to sit by me?"

Nutmeg immediately plopped down and put her head on Keith's leg.

I looked at them and shook my head. "Well, Chief, you sure have a way with the ladies."

"So you are telling me if I pat this spot on the other side of me you will sit down and lay your head on my leg?"

I put both hands on my hips. "No, I'm not telling you that. But I will sit next to you so I can see what goodies you brought with you."

Keith picked up the packet of papers and opened the folder. "As I told you, Renee Dover died in 1999 at the age of 22. Eight years later at the age of 30, she came back to life. Meanwhile, the fingerprints I put through the system today identifies the owner as Sadie Maxwell, Youngstown, Ohio.

"Sadie had a drinking problem which resulted in an accident which killed her husband and two children. It netted Sadie a million dollars in life insurance and six years in jail."

I leaned forward to get a better look at the papers he held in his hand. "Wow, that is quite a background. I didn't expect anything like that."

"Neither did I. Anyway, she served six years of a twelve year sentence for manslaughter. No one ever heard from her again. She took the money out of the bank in increments of thousands of dollars, but never opened another bank account in her own name."

"This is like a crime novel," I said.

"Oh, it gets better. Two years after Sadie Maxwell was released from prison, Renee Dover arose from the dead. Her social security card became active again. She opened bank accounts and had credit cards."

"Where does Margie Steever fit into this?" I asked.

"Margarette Mary Steever served time in the same prison as Sadie. Margarette didn't actually do anything. She was in the car when a girlfriend delivered drugs. It was back when they threw the book at you if you were anywhere around the crime.

"Margie got sentenced to 25 years to life. A judge reviewed the case and paroled her. She served 7 years. Maybe she and Renee were as close as sisters. You know family doesn't always have to be related."

"Amazing what you don't know about people when you see them walking down the street." I thought of my own life. I doubt anyone would believe my real father was a murderer or no one was sure what happened to my birth mother, or Emma kidnapped me. I did know my feelings for Emma had become so much deeper since she told me my life story.

CHAPTER 32

Keith and I were both quiet and lost in thought when his radio began to crackle. "Dispatch to Chief Wesley. Keith, are you there?"

"Sure, what's up?"

"There has been a shooting near Pier 63. One dead. Randy and Amanda are on their way and I contacted the coroner and Jess."

"Thanks. I'm on my way."

I was up at the word shooting. My boots were by the front door as was my coat. Keith had come in with nothing but his papers. "I guess this is a sign you want to come along?"

"Of course, I said. "Pier 63 is all the way on the other side of the lake near Route 13. It's the major road in and out of Moonstone Lake. Hardly a secluded place for a murder."

We drove up to a madhouse. People were milling

around. Randy's cruiser, Amanda's cruiser, the coroner's car, two ambulances and the CSI van were all parked at the end of the dock with lights flashing.

We walked out to the pier where all the commotion was. There were so many people, I didn't know if the wooden deck would hold much more weight.

The body already had a body bag on it. A woman I didn't recognize sat on the edge of the dock being tended to by an EMT. At the present time, he took her blood pressure. She didn't appear to be wounded.

Keith said nothing to anyone. He walked up to the body in the bag and unzipped it enough to identify it. Nutmeg and I were close enough to look over his shoulder when he bent down.

I let out an audible gasp. The cold dead body of Ronny Watts lay before me.

Ronny went to school with the rest of us but in a class two years ahead. He'd been on the City Council since he graduated from law school and moved back to Moonstone Lake.

I didn't think Ronny had any enemies. His law practice focused mostly on Imminent Domain issues. Few of those cases involved people from Moonstone Lake. Mostly his clients were from Stansfield and larger cities.

CHAPTER 33

What did it mean? Jackson Ramp's body had the same wound. A single gunshot wound to the forehead. We had the impression the shooter didn't have much experience.

Ronny Watts had a single wound smack in the center of his forehead. It changed what I thought about the Ramp murder. Maybe it didn't have anything to do with the women after all. Now the chore would be to see if the women and Ronny were connected in any way.

I looked around. The Sunshine Hotel and Water Park were about fifty yards to the left and maybe one hundred feet in front of the dock. There were boats moored on both sides of the pier. Many people from the lake drove their boats across the water to one of the several restaurants around the lake's perimeter.

It had warmed up all day, it reached a balmy forty-three degrees.

People were out walking, working on booths within rifle range of the pier, and campers sat on lounge chairs a half a block east at the campground and cabins.

The way I had it figured, any one of three hundred people could have shot Ronny.

Randy and Amanda were both questioning people who owned the boats. Jesse and his CSI team held bright lights and scoured the water around the pier and the plank floor of the dock, one board at a time.

I saw Margie, Ashly and the three kids standing at the end of the sidewalk to the right of the dock. I made it a point not to make eye contact with any of them.

A thought popped into my head. We now had one less suspect. Timothy Clark still occupied a cell at the police station.

CHAPTER 34

Keith, Amanda and Randy had their heads together discussing something. I knew I could walk over to them and listen, but I thought better of it.

They broke up their little conference and Keith came toward me.

"Amanda and Randy think it was a random sniper. I might agree. Someone said it's Ronny Watts' wife sitting on the dock. Do you know her?"

"Not really; I didn't even recognize her when we walked up. He got married after law school and before they moved to Moonstone Lake. I think her name is Ruth."

We started toward the woman when Keith's radio came to life again. "Keith, a passerby reported a dead body on the south side of the lake at the West edge of the Boardwalk."

"You mean by the police station?"

"Yes, I do. I can see the crowd gathering if I look out the front door."

"Ok. I'll be right there."

He looked at me. "The interview with Ronny's wife will have to wait. There is another shooting on the south side, extremely close to the police station. I believe whoever is shooting people isn't afraid they will get caught."

Keith put two fingers in his mouth and whistled. The shrill sound made everyone look his way. He motioned for his officers, Jess, the coroner and an EMT to come his way. "There has been another shooting over by the police station. I'd like for a crew to go over there without causing a panic. I have no idea what is going on."

No one said a word. They stood quietly with what I describe as total shock on their faces. Jess Morgan, the CSI director broke the silence. "Keith, I know this is your show, but I think you should stay here. It will cause a lot of questions if you leave the scene so soon." He nodded at the coroner. "Phil." He tapped one of the EMT's on the shoulder. "We can go. As soon as we see what is going on, we will let you know."

Keith agreed and the men left, acting like they were in no particular hurry.

I heard a slight wail of an ambulance and realized another buggy had been dispatched to the other crime scene.

Four reserve officers were now on duty every night until the festival ended. I looked at my phone, eleven o'clock. At around three a.m. four replacements would be on the grounds. I wondered if I should mention it to Keith or stay out of his way. I decided to chance it. "Keith, may I speak to you a minute?"

He took a few steps away from the area and looked me in the eye. "What?"

"It dawned on me the four men you have here now will have replacements in a few hours. Maybe they could come early and help talk to the witnesses, if there are any."

He put his hand on my shoulder. "Great idea. Can you take care of it for me. Just call dispatch. Ask for the Highway Patrol and some Sheriff's deputies to join us also."

Within twenty minutes, the area swarmed with additional troops. They set up a command post under a canopy in front of one of the food trucks.

Once every one of the extras had a specific job. Keith and I left quietly with no lights and sirens and headed for the second shooting.

"Anyone we know?" Keith asked, as we walked up. "Unfortunately, yes. It's Seth Diamond."

Seth Diamond had been delivering milk in Moonstone Lake since I was a kid. Why him?

Someone had placed a sheet over Seth. When Keith pulled it back, I saw an unmistakable gunshot in the center of his forehead. The exact same wound as Ronny Watts and Jackson Ramp.

It got more and more certain the women, Renee, Margie, Alice and Ruth, no matter how sordid their pasts, did not kill any of these people.

A chill went through me. As of an hour ago, Moonstone Lake was no longer the safe, beautiful place I knew my entire life.

CHAPTER 35

Hours later, everyone within a mile of either scene had been questioned. Yellow tape remained around both areas, and Moonstone Lake again seemed tranquil.

Nutmeg and I didn't get to bed until seven a.m. As a matter of fact, I didn't bother to lay down. I took a long hot shower, put on flannel-lined jeans, added a heather gray Henley under my fleece lined top and wore heavy socks with Sketcher boots. Even though the temperature was mild, I was cold all over.

Not only did I feed Nutmeg her dog food, but when I ordered a ham and cheese omelet from the kitchen, I ordered one for her also.

I took it to the front and laid it down where she could reach it. I leaned against the hostess station and ate mine while I talked to Aunt Sandy. "I guess you heard about the shootings last night?"

"I'd venture to say, by ten o'clock, the entire area will know about them." She held a copy of the Moonstone Reflection, the Stanfield Gazette, and the St. Louis Star. The front page of all of them made some reference to the shootings.

But the thing that caught my eye had nothing to do with the killings. Although we were mentioned in a corner of the Star, the main story featured Daniel Wade Demount and the arrest of those involved in an extortion ring plaguing him for the past ten years.

It told about how a child would accuse Demount of improper advances. The child's parents would settle for an unknown amount of money and they would kick back a large portion to Demount's manager.

It took the FBI, according to the story, nine years to figure out how it was done. The only constant in the case came when the children, questioned alone, couldn't come up with one bad thing about Demount's treatment of them.

The dozen children involved were all age six or seven at the time of the incidents. Demount said he either stayed with them because they failed to get on their bus after the show or he found them wandering around the studio lots.

Demount's manager, Dustin James, has been under surveillance for several years before the pattern emerged.

Daniel Demount wasn't charged with a crime but the studio let him go this week stating he caused too much disgrace due to no fault of his own.

They bought out the rest of his contract for 2.3 million dollars.

Dustin James faces twelve counts of embezzlement, fraud and theft. It is thought over the years James netted over 100 million dollars, some of which he shared with the parents of the children involved.

Each parent is being questioned to see if they were a part of the scheme or innocent pawns.

The network announced they will be looking for a new Wrangler Jim in the near future. For now, the set will remain closed pending the outcome of the Dustin James case.

It is not clear if anyone else at the network was involved.

Adios, Wrangler Jim.

I read it out loud and Aunt Sandy wasn't quite sure what to make of it. Quickly I explained how Keith and I were sure the Demount case and the killing of Jackson Ramp were intertwined.

Unless the killings of Seth Diamond and Ronny Watts happened to be a way to throw us off track, we were completely wrong.

CHAPTER 36

Except for the article Liz Austin wrote for the Moonstone Lake Reflection, it sounded as though we had a mad killer on the loose.

Liz only told the facts as we knew them and didn't sensationalize the events.

Of course, newspapers wanted to sell copies. Liz wanted to tell the story and stay loyal to the town she grew up in and loved.

"I'd better get to work," I said. "There are at least a hundred entries to our cooking contest already. I hope they are not all for the same category."

Before Aunt Sandy and I had time to talk anymore, a group of five men came in. Their topic of conversation was the killings. I heard one man say he didn't want his wife to stay and sell her wares. "Isn't worth it if she gets shot," he said.

"I told my wife and kids to stay off the streets until they catch this psychopath. I never thought I'd see anything like this in Moonstone Lake. We chose to raise our kids here because it has always been so safe."

The rest of their words faded as they were seated.

I felt as if someone had kicked me in the stomach. The last thing I wanted was to be afraid in my own home town, but I had to admit, I didn't want Mother and her friends wandering all over town until whoever was trying to ruin our lives was caught.

CHAPTER 37

I went back by the cheesecake truck and asked the owner if he had a sandwich bag I could have.

He gave me one, and I carefully put a piece of blue cloth inside and sealed it. At the point in my walk where I turned off the main path and headed toward the Boardwalk, I heard a loud *pop*.

People began to scatter and take cover behind buildings and benches. I was no exception. Nutmeg and I ducked behind the Gray Goose, the business next door to us, and hugged the back of the buildings until we reached the rear kitchen door of the café.

I pounded hard until someone opened it.

Jose, one of the line cooks, peeked out. When he saw me he asked, "Miss Arizona, what is going on out there? About fifty people have run into the dining room in the last five minutes. Are you all right?"

"Yes, I'm fine. We need to call 911."

"I don't think so," he said. "There are already three police cars in Granny's Bed and Breakfast parking lot and several other official vehicles."

"Thanks," I said, as I scooted by him and walked toward the dining room.

He didn't exaggerate. It was standing room only in there. I made my way to the front. "Is it another shooting?" I asked Lewis and Aunt Sandy who stood side by side at the front window.

"I think so," Lewis said. "I guess instead of standing here being a sightseer, we should try to calm these folks down with some coffee and normalcy."

I wanted so much to go out and see what happened and if I knew the victim, but I stayed inside and tried to listen to as many conversations as I could and keep people seated and calm with coffee and soft drinks.

My phone rang nearly an hour later. Keith's picture flashed on the screen. "Hi, I only have a minute. Another shooting. This woman wasn't from town. She was a crafter from Wisconsin. Her name is Arlene Mann. Her husband said they have had a homemade soap booth for the past twenty-four years. Okay. Gotta go."

He hung up before I even had a chance to say *hello.*

Three people shot to death in Moonstone Lake, nine days before the opening of the festival. I knew it would be a bad day. This time the shooter killed his or her victim in broad daylight.

I walked to the back where the coffee pots were getting a workout. "Benny, please fix about ten cups of coffee to go and run it over to Granny's."

He gave me a hesitant look. "I'm sorry, Benny. If you don't want to go out, I understand. I also believe if the killer is going to kill again today, he will move to a location far away from this one.

"Tell you what, you fix it and I'll take it."

"Will you be upset with me?" he asked.

"Oh, my goodness, no. I understand completely."

I took the coffee over and sat it on the fender of Amanda's cruiser. She looked my way. When I pointed to her car, she gave me a thumbs up.

One of the conversations I overheard stuck with me the rest of the day. Two men were in a booth close to mine in the back. I'd set down to wait for more coffee to brew. I didn't know either of them.

Man one - "How long has this festival of theirs been going on?

Man two - "At least twenty-years."

Man one- "Maybe it was time to slow them down."

Man two- "What do you mean by slow them down? We been coming here since the kids were little. I always enjoy it."

Man one - "I know for sure Jeffrey Holmes has met with the committee here many times trying to get them to cut the length of the festival so other towns can enrich their coffers too.

"Between the summer tourists here and the winter festival taking up six weeks, no one is doing any business but Moonstone Lake."

Man two – "I think that's pretty petty myself. If

someone puts in as much work as these people do, they should be able to reap the reward."

Man one – "It ain't just Shining Star Lake, it's the snow slopes in the Boston Mountains, and three or four more places I can't think of at the moment."

Man two – "Sounds like sour grapes to me. There are hundreds of ways to bring tourists to your town. Branson, Missouri has country music, St. Charles has antiques, I could name a dozen."

Man one- "I'm just saying there were ways to help others be successful. It didn't have to come to this."

Man two – "I need to move on. It you think these killings are because of the success of Moonstone Lake, then I think there are some sick people out there."

A couple came up to me a little later. The woman asked, "If I don't feel safe entering your cooking contest, can I have my entry fee back?"

Another, "They aren't going to be able to stop whoever is killing people. There are already sixteen hundred extra people in town with booths and food trucks. Wait until another ten thousand a day start filing through to buy and sightsee. It'll be a sniper's paradise."

CHAPTER 38

After work I took Nutmeg out through the kitchen door. She walked around, did her business and came right back.

Lewis had his hat and coat, ready to leave for the night. "Are you afraid?" I asked him.

"I don't know if you would call it afraid or cautious. I have a taxi picking me up at the back door. I'll miss my walks, but I owe it to my wife and kids to be careful. I notice you and Nutmeg aren't doing your nightly run."

"I feel like you do. It would be different if I knew why the sniper wanted to kill people. Maybe I wouldn't fit his profile and I might be safe. As it is, I will lift weights until this is over." As he slipped into his coat I said, "Can I ask you something?"

"Sure."

"I overheard a conversation today. They said it

might be someone trying to shut down the festival. They said we hogged the tourist trade with the lake traffic in the summer and the festival for an entire six weeks in the winter. Do you think there could be any truth to that?"

"It could be. I read once the most common reasons for murder are love, jealousy, financial gain, hate and vengeance. I'll add one more, because the person has a screw loose."

I heard the taxi horn. Lewis leaned over and kissed the top of my forehead. "Please be careful. Let the police handle this. I know you like to help Keith, but what is going on here is especially depraved. To randomly kill people you don't know takes a special kind of monster."

I'm not jumpy or unusually nervous most of the time. This night I walked back to the door Lewis left through and made sure it was locked.

On my way past the refrigerator, I took a piece of pumpkin pie and a scoop of whipped cream.

We always left a light on in every area of the restaurant. Tonight I was especially glad there were no dark corners.

CHAPTER 39

I hadn't heard from Keith since his one phone call earlier in the day. Also, I hadn't heard any more sirens or seen any flashing red lights.

Moonstone Lake Café and Sunday Brunch sat in the middle of the block on the north side of the Boardwalk.

Old Cove Road ran behind us, and on the other side of it lay the sidewalk that skirted the lake.

On our side of the street were seventeen businesses. We were the sixth one from the West. The Boardwalk was just that, a wide street with ornate gas lamps for street lights and wrought iron benches.

The south side of the street also had seventeen specialty shops including a bakery, a taco bar and a beer garden. Old Cobblestone Lane ran behind that side and on the far side of it sat a grocery store, a drug store, and the Goodwill Store.

Behind those the residential area began. Most of the owners of the shops on the Boardwalk lived on this side of the lake.

The north side of the lake had all the other townsfolk, a liquor store, the Sunshine Hotel and Water Park and downtown which included the Courthouse and the town square.

I could look out my second story window and see the town was quiet. I hoped nothing else would happen.

CHAPTER 40

By eleven o'clock I had done a load of laundry and cleaned my bathroom. I was still wide awake. I couldn't get my mind off of what the man said. In so many words, he said the town tried to keep all the business here.

My weights were in the closet. I pulled out five pound and seven pound pairs, put my workout sheet on the kitchen table and proceeded to take my mind off the killings by working up a sweat.

I washed my face, brushed my teeth and took my computer to bed with me. Nutmeg rested with her head on my knee. It looked as if she were watching the monitor.

In the search bar I typed *Fall and Winter Festivals within one hundred miles of Moonstone Lake.*

Nine towns came up. I eliminated the three

farthest away. Then I took away three I knew had City Fairs in the spring or fall based around livestock animals. One had a rodeo, which left two. Shooting Star Lake and Mountain View, one to our east about fifty miles and one to the south about thirty miles.

I Googled Mountain View. They had a successful local light display put on by a collaboration of the local civic clubs. This would be their thirtieth year. They were well into a Christmas tradition before we began ours. Once I saw the pictures of Mountain View's light show on the website, I realized I had seen it before.

The last one, Shining Star Lake, was mentioned in the conversation I'd overheard earlier in the day.

Chapter 41

Shining Star Lake had a larger population than Moonstone Lake. We boasted twenty-four hundred permanent residents. Shining Star had thirty-one hundred. To my mind, if they wanted a Christmas festival or a light display, they had enough people to sustain it even if only the townspeople visited. Mom said when our light festival began, we had ten craft booths, two food trucks and a light display fashioned by the janitor at the high school.

Shining Star Lake had a professional website. It went on and on about the fishing at the lake and the fifteen or so tournaments an ardent fisherman could enter throughout the year.

Everything in the town had a fishing theme. The motels and cabins listed looked masculine; the restaurants definitely catered to the male. Almost all of them had Saloon, Bar, or Beer in their names.

Other than a grocery store, liquor store and tobacco shop, most of the stores near the lake catered to fishermen and outdoorsmen.

I didn't see it as a family destination. If they indeed failed at a winter pageant, it didn't have anything to do with Moonstone Lake's Festival of Lights and its success.

I took off early to pay a visit to Shining Star Lake and to get a feel for its ambiance.

Aunt Sandy, Mom and I shared a car. We really didn't need one, but none of us liked to beg for a ride to go to one of the nearby cities to shop or visit a dentist or a doctor, so we kept one in the garage at the back of the property.

Nutmeg loved to ride. She sat up front and looked out the window the entire time. I stopped several times along the way to photograph the scenery. When we reached the sign noting one mile to Shining Star Lake, we began to climb a hill.

At the top we were graced with one of the most beautiful scenes I'd had the good fortune to gaze upon.

The lake sat at the bottom of a canyon. No homes were built on its shores and all the boats were tied to piers in inlets all around it.

It could only be called spectacular.

I'd brought a notepad with me and jotted down my first observation. It appeared the only road in and out of the town happened to be the steep hill we climbed to reach it. I wanted to explore because I couldn't believe people had to navigate the hill every time they left town. It would be a nightmare with the slightest amount of snow or ice.

The only way down to the lake lay before us. A long narrow, curvy road with no shoulder visible on either side.

Considering the winters we had in this part of the country, I could see why many people would not want to come here during the snowy season.

I didn't have binoculars so I used my telephoto lens to scan the area. As gorgeous as the land appeared to be, in my opinion, the only kind of festival or fair this town could support would have to be in the summertime.

Nutmeg ran around the car a few times and hopped back in. Time to see what else we could find out.

One main street ran straight through the town and around the perimeter of the lake which was about half the size of Moonstone Lake. Streets with names like Guppy Lane, Walleye Road and Trout Circle went to the right and up hills to residential neighborhoods.

I pulled in to what I thought to be a convenience store and gas station. The left side served as a marina and the other side a gas station.

A woman in her forties dressed in a faded man's shirt and a baggy pair of jeans greeted me. "Well, hello there, young lady. Are you lost?"

Nutmeg jumped out and ran to a wooden porch lined with rocking chairs and two checker boards sitting on stumps.

"No. I've lived in this area all my life and have never ventured in this direction. Today is a beautiful day to do a little sightseeing."

"I know you, don't I?" she said.

"Depends, ever been to Moonstone Lake?"

"Why yes, you have the restaurant, right?"

"One of them, yes."

"Come on in. Have a cold drink." She laughed. "Maybe today, a warm drink would be better."

"Do you have any coffee?" I asked.

"Sure." She pointed to a small table near the front window. "You have a seat and I'll get us a cup."

I took off my coat and picked a sunny place to sit. I tried to think of a way to approach the subject of a festival. She saved me the trouble. "We have a van full of men who go over there every day. It is extra work right now. The fishing trade is slow in the winter. We tried a light festival.

"We never had enough people to make a go of it. Every one of the crafters, even the ones from here, want to go to your festival."

"The people who put it on have been doing it for twenty-five years," I said. "They know what they are doing. I'm not involved in the planning of it."

"I hear there's been some trouble over there the last few nights. A sniper, I hear."

"Yes, who would do a thing like that? Who kills people they don't even know?" I asked.

She didn't answer. Someone drove up to one of the gas pumps and she went out to help them. I took the opportunity to leave. As Nutmeg and I got in the car, she waved and said, "Come back again."

I waved back.

Nutmeg and I drove up to the top of one of the residential streets and down another. It seemed as though the further we got away from town the nicer the homes were.

I had to agree the town wasn't nearly as prosperous as Moonstone Lake. Immediately I was ashamed of myself. I had no right to judge a town for what I saw on one winter's day. It might be a real happening place come spring.

On my third trip through the neighborhoods, I found a paved two-lane road. On my phone I looked up the name of it, Marlin Freeway. I followed the road on the map with my finger. After twenty miles or so a secondary road branched off and wound around until it met up with Lake Road 313, the one we drove in on.

So if you were coming from the north, you could use the freeway. Problem was, there were no small towns. For at least eighty miles there were only tiny towns and villages. Most likely they were nothing more than a local store and a gas station.

We found a town square with quaint houses on the streets projecting off it. There were huge shade trees. Many people were outside sitting at tables and benches at the businesses directly around the square.

I pictured it as a wonderful sight-seeing destination were it not for the roads.

Chapter 42

We parked in one of the pull offs and got out to look at the lake. The water was crystal clear. I could see fish. Small ones swam close to the shore and a little bit bigger ones farther out as the water got deeper.

There were cute signs all the way around the lake.

ANGELS
WHO GUARD YOU
WHEN YOU DRIVE
USUALLY
RETIRE AT
65
BURMA SHAVE

I'd heard about Burma Shave signs since my

childhood. This is the first time I'd ever seen one. I stopped at each one and tried to get all of the ones included in the same sign into one photograph.

IT'S BEST FOR
ONE WHO HITS
THE BOTTLE
TO LET ANOTHER
USE THE THROTTLE
BURMA SHAVE

A MAN   A MISS
A CAR   A CURVE
HE KISSED THE MISS
AND MISSED THE CURVE
BURMA SHAVE

YOU CAN DRIVE
A MILE A MINUTE
BUT THERE IS NO
FUTURE IN IT
BURMA SHAVE

I laughed out loud. I knew others would not think the signs as entertaining as I did, but I intended to hang them somewhere in the café.

As the sun began to dip below the edge of the canyon, I thought we'd best head for home.

We were nearly to the top of the hill when a van began driving down toward the lake. The driver got within fifty yards of us and made no attempt to pull over or slow down.

I stopped.

He stopped.

Slowly I moved as close to the edge as I could without sliding down the steep incline into a stand of pine trees several feet below me.

The van didn't move.

My hands were sweaty and shaking, my body tensed as I opened my car door. "Hi," I yelled. "I don't think there is room for both of us on this road. Maybe if you move over to your left some more, I can get by. I have the smallest vehicle."

A man got out of the driver's side and another out of the passenger's side of the van. "I think the best thing for everyone, sweetheart, is for you to back down the hill and let us go home."

I moved a bit and nearly slid off the side of the unpaved road. "But sir, I am only a few feet from the top. It would be easier for you to back up and let me pass."

The strangest thing happened. At the bottom of the hill stood the Lady in Red. She didn't move, she only stood perfectly still. It looked like she was watching what would happen next.

The man walked toward me and when he got within a few feet, he looked over the side and down into the trees. "Looks like a difficult drive for an inexperienced driver."

Nutmeg had crawled over to the driver's side and jumped out of the car. She began to growl.

"If that dog comes any closer to me, I will kick her down the ridge."

I looked down the hill to see if the Lady in Red

went for help or maybe would come up and help us herself. She no longer stood there. A quick glance around told me she was gone.

There were no vehicles on the streets and no people on the sidewalks.

The sliding door of the van opened and two more men stepped out. One said, "Leave her alone, Red, it's getting late. Let her pass."

The man on the other side walked up closer and said, "Red, David's right. Let the girl pass. You know there is room. I'm cold and tired."

The one they called Red spoke up. "Don't you know who this is? It's the lady from the restaurant in Moonstone Lake. It isn't bad enough they ruin our lives from there, now they are coming here."

I wanted to say something but I knew my voice would crack and I didn't want the man to know how scared I was. Nutmeg stepped closer and bared her teeth. I tried to call her back but I knew she would rather die than let me get hurt.

"What did I tell you about the dog?" he said. He walked back to the van and pulled a billy club from under the seat.

The two men from the back seats walked up beside him. "Enough, young lady, get in your car. Red is going to let you pass. Then he walked over to the driver's side of the van, started it and moved it as far to the right as he could while the second man guided him.

Nutmeg and I got into our car and we passed them with barely an inch to spare.

When I got to the main road, I drove about a half mile before I pulled over and cried. I hadn't been so afraid in ages.

As unpleasant as the man called Red was, I couldn't, in my heart, believe someone would kill people over a winter festival.

Nutmeg snuggled up next to me and licked my face. I took several deep breaths and headed for home.

Chapter 43

When I drove up to the garage, the only lights on in the restaurant were the security lights. Thank goodness we had a dusk-to-dawn light on both sides of the garage and the inside light came on as the door opened.

Once I put the car away, I had two choices to get into my apartment. I could unlock the service door, go down the outside hall and push my code into the door between the café and the apartment building.

I decided to walk around the building to the front and go inside from there. It might not have been my best choice. As I came around the corner of the building, I saw Keith sitting on the bench under the Hackberry tree to the left of the front door.

His posture told me he was not happy. His legs were straight out in front of him with his heels on the sidewalk and his toes pointed toward the sky.

Both arms were crossed over his chest and the ball cap he wore, with the word, POLICE, in two-inch white letters covered his forehead all the way to his eyebrows.

Nutmeg barked and ran to him, tail wagging. He reached down and gave the dog a pat on the head and put both hands on his hips. "Where have you been?"

His voice held an edge I hadn't heard since we sparred for a few weeks when he first moved to Moonstone Lake.

"I took the day off," I said, vaguely.

He walked toward me, and when he stood close enough, he put one hand on each of my shoulders. "Did you miss the activity in town the last few days? The part where someone is sneaking around killing our residents?"

"Sure, I know about it. I didn't have to worry. I wasn't in town."

"No, you weren't. You took it upon yourself to go looking for clues in Shining Star Lake."

"How do you know?" I asked.

"Because I got a phone call from a woman there who said you'd been in town and when you tried to leave, some men gave you a hard time."

"I guess my question is, why would someone call you? There is little you could do from here. Why didn't she call the local PD?"

"Arizona, they don't have a police department. The Highway Patrol is there a couple of times a week to answer complaints. Mostly it's a lawless town."

"Oh, come on, this isn't the Ole Wild West.

Everyone has law in this day and age."

"No, Ary, they don't. Actually, the Annual Festival of Lights is one of the main reasons our police department is so good. Moonstone Lake has enough tax revenue to fund all of it. I don't believe you saw much thriving business on your visit today."

He let go of my shoulders and took a step back and looked down toward Nutmeg. "It's a good thing you have Nutmeg to protect you. Red Korte is a bad man. Most people know to stay away from him." Keith nearly fell onto the bench behind him. He lowered his head and covered his face with both hands. After a long moment he looked up. "Arizona, since I received the call, I called and texted you over and over again. I'm sure the Highway Patrol is there now. But why didn't you answer? The pictures flooding my mind are not something I care to repeat."

I took the phone out of my jacket pocket and looked at it. There were indeed several messages from Mom, Aunt Sandy and Keith. When I retrieved my phone, the plastic bag with the piece of cloth I took from Nutmeg the other night fell on the ground.

Keith picked it up but didn't hand it back to me.

"Do you think Red Korte is the shooter?" I asked. "The baggie you have in your hand is a piece of a shirt I took from Nutmeg after she chased someone the other night."

"I don't know what to think. He, along with all the other residents of Shining Star Lake, know they are the prime suspects. For years there has been grumbling from there about how unfair it is Moonstone Lake has most of the tourist trade, summer and winter.

"We have no idea who it is. Today we searched everyone coming into town and leaving. It is most likely why he gave you a hard time. He has a rap sheet as long as your arm. Thing is, none of it is for crimes of violence.

"He is a thief, writes bad checks, and harasses people, and he is really good at selling to one person what he stole from another. He has never gone so far as to hurt anyone. The Festival committee is going to announce a large reward for information about the killings."

I sat on the bench and scooted close to him. "I didn't mean to upset you. Some men came into the restaurant and pretty much said someone from Shining Star Lake was the sniper. I couldn't understand how they could blame an entire town for their successes and failures.

"Nutmeg and I rode over there. It's only thirty miles. The scenery on the way there kept me mesmerized and I stopped several times to take pictures.

"I don't know if you have been there, but you have to go up a big hill to get into town. It's not just any hill, it's more like a San Francisco hill.

"I won't bore you with any more details. The bottom line is, I stayed too long and then Red and a van full of his friends were coming home from working here at the festival grounds, and they wouldn't let me pass." I put my hand on his arm. "I'm so sorry, I didn't think. I won't do anything like that again."

"What makes it worse, Ary, is you didn't tell your aunt or your mother or anyone else where you were going."

He turned toward me. "I guess I didn't realize how much I really cared about you until I couldn't find you." He stood and pulled me up to him. "Please, don't do anything like this again."

He kissed me hard and I kissed him back. "I won't," I said, in a near whisper. "I'm not trying to make light of this situation, but should we be sitting out here in the open with a sniper roaming around?" I didn't mean to smile but I couldn't help it.

He pushed me back and looked at me. "You're incorrigible, you know."

"Yes, I know."

Chapter 44

I didn't really want to get into the details of my day with Mom and Aunt Sandy, but I couldn't let them stew and worry all night.

Since Mother's apartment was on the first floor, I stopped by there first. I tapped on the door.

"It's about time I heard from you," she said, as she opened the door. "Where have you been all day?"

I stepped past her and went into her apartment. It looked like a Christmas toy warehouse. "I went to Shining Star Lake. I've heard talk they blame Moonstone Lake for their lack of growth. A trip over there showed me they are wrong.

"Their infrastructure, or lack of, is their reason for failure. I can't imagine anyone wanting to drive a food truck or a trailer full of goods up and down the hill to set up for a craft show."

Mom sat in the recliner facing the TV which wasn't on. "Oh, they have been spouting the same old song and dance for the last twenty-years.

"The only people who are going to visit there regularly are the avid fishermen and hunters with their four-wheel-drive trucks.

"Mary Christiansen, and about half of the festival committee, went over to visit them and help them set up a light display. The town looked beautiful, it snowed five inches the night they were supposed to open. Snow stayed on the ground until after New Year's.

"I don't think they had but a handful of visitors. Even the townsfolk had problems with the roads. You're lucky you didn't run into Red Korte."

I sat on the couch. "But I did. I drove up the hill and was maybe five feet from the top when he and a van full of men began to drive down it. He said I'd have to back down the hill and let him go home before I could leave."

She reached down for Nutmeg, who sat as close to Mom's chair as she could. "I bet you didn't like that, did you, girl?" Nutmeg barked and we laughed. "Did you back down?"

"No, another man got out of the back of the van, went around to the driver's side and let me get by them."

"It must have been Dwayne Osborn. Red wouldn't let anyone else get by with it. I'm glad you are okay. Stop by and talk to Aunt Sandy. She has been pacing with worry for hours."

"I will. Are you ready for the show? It begins in three days."

"We are ready. We decided we will be safe if we stay in the tents. I wish they would catch the crazy person who is responsible for the shootings."

"We all do, Mom. You be careful."

"You, too. Don't be so eager to help catch a killer. If he finds out you are looking for him, he might come after you."

She walked me to the door but before she opened it she said, "Something has been bothering me. The first five years of the festival, we had a carnival. It consisted of a walkway of games of chance and a Ferris Wheel."

"I didn't know that. Why don't we have one now?"

"That is why I'm telling you this. On the last day of the festival, New Year's Day, one of the seats on the Ferris Wheel snapped off and a young man and woman fell out. The boy was killed, but the girl managed to hold on until a man from another car was able to get hold of her.

"The boy's father swore one day he would be back and make the town pay for what we did to his son.

"Of course we had nothing to do with it. His family moved away, and I've been racking my brain to come up with his name. You might ask your Aunt Sandra if she remembers who he was.

"It is nearly twenty-years and he probably didn't mean it anyway. But, ever since the first shooting, the incident came to mind.

"It might only be the memories of an old lady."

We said good-bye and I left to make my next visit.

CHAPTER 45

Aunt Sandy had an uncanny habit of opening her door before I had a chance to knock. She had Blynkin in her arms but put him down to hug me. "My goodness, Arizona, you are going to make me old before my time if you don't stop disappearing."

"You act like I do it all the time. I only took a day off, took pictures, lost track of time, let my phone battery go down and got home late. That is about all there is to it." I hoped it served as a good enough explanation and I wouldn't have to repeat what I told Mom.

"Are you hungry?" she asked.

"No, actually, I feel grimy and tired. There is a hot bath in my near future. Then to bed. I'm not hungry for the first time in a long time.

"I do have one question, though. Mom told me a man's son fell and was killed on a Ferris Wheel that used to be at the festival. Do you remember his name?"

"Sure I do. I happened to be on the wheel that night. Our seat had reached the bottom and was about the third one going back up when I saw what happened. It's not something I will ever forget.

"The boy was Larry, well, Lawrence Eastburn, Jr. He had turned eighteen the day before and had already enlisted in the Marines. The men in this family always joined the Marines.

"I remember all the men were big and Larry's mother barely came up to his shoulder. Nice guy, nice family. His family filed a lawsuit against the city for millions of dollars.

"The Ferris Wheel owner was found negligent and went to jail for a few years. Larry's father still insisted the town was at fault. He went so far as to threaten to kill us all."

"I hope he isn't making good on his promise," I said.

"I doubt it. They only stayed in town about six months after the accident. I never heard another thing about it. The boy's buried in the Moonstone Lake Cemetery. I've heard someone sends flowers every Memorial Day in remembrance. Surely it couldn't be Larry Senior after all of these years."

"Surely not." I repeated, but I wasn't convinced.

CHAPTER 46

By the time I fed Nutmeg, relaxed in a hot bath and got my pjs on, I could hardly hold my eyes open. I had to be at work early. Aunt Sandy and I were going to decorate the overflow room and transform it into a contestant's home base and a place for the judges to sit while they tasted the food.

I got five super soft and comfy chairs from Logan's Furniture downtown. They donated them for the duration of the contest.

We had two six-foot tables to go in front of the chairs for the judges to taste the food. Each judge had a printed name plaque with his name, job, or position printed on it.

Mary Stanley, from the rental company furnished the tablecloths and skirts for the tables.

All of those items were on the right side of the room. On the left there were twelve places for the cooks and their dishes. The entries were dated and time stamped, and the first dozen people who signed up in each category could participate.

It was too much to ask the judges to taste thirty or more plates of food and try to remember the subtle differences between them.

We had no more than put the last touches on it when Liz Austin showed up with her camera and notebook. "I want to take some pictures for tomorrow's paper. How about a few of just the room and then some with you two?" She nodded toward Aunt Sandy and me.

While she took the pictures of the room sans people, I went to the kitchen to fetch Lewis who had done most of the work to set the whole thing up.

We had Liz interview Lewis and we watched. He was a natural.

He had the contest schedule.

Sunday: Salad
Monday: Soup
Tuesday: Appetizer
Wednesday: One pot main dish
Thursday: Dessert
Friday: Awards and Prizes
Saturday: Dinner for all winners.

Each contestant had been issued six passes to get in the door the night their dish would be judged. We wished we could open the place up to the entire town, but it would be crowded anyway with twelve contestants, five judges, the staff and the eighty-four guests if they all showed up.

We were short-handed in the evening, and I

waited tables and bussed them. Everyone loved it when I worked in a position where I earned tips. I split them between all the dining room help on the shift. I didn't keep any of it for myself.

Some people over tipped me because I was the boss. Others didn't tip me at all for the same reason.

Several people, throughout the day, commented about there not being a shooting for two days. I hoped it continued.

No such luck. We had no sooner locked the doors than we heard sirens heading to the north side of the lake.

The patrons who were still eating didn't want to go out, and people on the street wanted in.

We tried to please everyone. With the kitchen closed, I offered soft drinks, iced tea and coffee at no charge, and all of the staff still in the café visited with people.

CHAPTER 47

I wanted to go to the North side and see what happened. Nutmeg and I hugged the buildings as we did to get home in the first place. When we arrived at the craft portion of the grounds, we went from the dark side of one tent to the dark and shadowy side of the next.

Nearly immediately in front of the Sunshine Hotel, lay the body of a man. He wore a business suit. Coroner Chad Baker leaned over the body. It had been at least three hours since we heard the commotion from the shooting.

Keith looked up. He'd been deep in conversation with a middle aged woman in a pretty blue dress with blood smeared on it. I didn't need to be a detective to figure out she and the dead man had been together.

He glared at me. Honestly, I expected as much. I

knew he wanted me to stay home, warm and safe. It wasn't in my DNA to stay in the background. I walked up and stood next to, and a little behind, him.

"Mrs. Gregg," I heard him say, "there is nothing any of us can do right now. Please go with Officer Wade. She will take you back to your room at the hotel, help you notify your family, and she will stay with you until someone gets here."

Gently he took the woman by the elbow and helped her over to Amanda's side. He smiled a sad smile at her and said, "I can't begin to tell you how sorry I am about John."

John Gregg. I put the name together in my mind, but it didn't set off any bells or whistles. I had no idea who he or she was.

Keith turned around and took me by the elbow, I might add, not as gently as he did with Mrs. Gregg. "What are you doing here?'

"The same thing as you," I said, "trying to put an end to these killings."

"Arizona, it has only been a few hours since you got home from playing detective at Shining Star Lake. Don't you ever get tired?"

"Of course I do. I wanted to tell you something."

"Unless it has something directly to do with John Gregg and his wife, it will have to wait a little while." I must have had a look he couldn't read because he let go of me and said, "I'm sorry, Ary. This is the fourth murder, and I hold my breath every time they call me praying it isn't anyone I know.

"That might sound callous, but I hardly keep

from passing out until I know it isn't someone I care about.

"I don't think that came out right. I care about all of the victims."

I put my hand in his. "I knew what you meant. And I know it was probably foolish to come here, but I think I have a lead, and I wanted you to be able to ask people who have lived here a long time if they know the story."

He walked away from the crowd, never letting go of my hand. "What is it?"

"Twenty years ago, the festival had a Ferris wheel and a street full of carnival games. On the last day of the celebration, a seat broke away and an eighteen-year-old boy fell to his death. His father promised one day he would come back here and kill the people of Moonstone Lake he felt were responsible."

"It could be," he said, "but twenty years is a long time to hold a grudge. We'll talk about it in the morning. Right now, I wish you would go home where it is safe. Please."

He motioned for Randy to come to him. "Randy, please escort Arizona home. By the way, I see your girlfriend is still here taking pictures. I'm sure she has enough. Even if she doesn't, I want her to leave."

Keith meant Liz Austin who had been dating Randy Malone for nearly a year.

He leaned down and kissed my cheek. "I am really interested. Some people can hold a grudge for a lifetime. We'll look into it tomorrow. I'll try to make breakfast."

Liz rode up front with Randy, and Nutmeg and I were in the back. I couldn't actually hear the conversation up there so I didn't try to be part of it.

I sat back and watched the few people who were out hustle down streets, stay next to buildings and keep their eyes on the rooftops of the nearby buildings.

The Lady in Red stood in front of a store and watched me go by. I made up my mind, the next time I saw her, I would follow her until I caught up with her. Nutmeg would help me.

Chapter 48

I didn't pay attention to the time. When Liz and I arrived back at the apartments, I went on inside so she and Randy could have a little privacy. I doubted they had had any more time together than Keith and I had since these killings began.

Nutmeg drank an entire bowl of water and ate three treats. Once she was satisfied, she jumped up on the couch and lay down.

I knew she could read my mind. It was the wee hours of the morning, yet she knew I would stay up awhile longer.

I looked up the local news stories from the winter of 2001. I didn't have to search long. The papers within two hundred miles of Moonstone Lake recounted the story. Pictures showed the Ferris wheel before and after the accident.

The entire right side of the car, where the boy

sat, broke, and I could tell there was nothing he could do.

There were interviews with the other people on the ride including my aunt Sandy. These articles ran for days. Larry's father was irate, which I understand, but he threatened to kill townspeople until they had to put him in custody for a few days.

When he got out, he filed suit against Moonstone Lake for thirty-million dollars and the carnival company for ten-million.

According to the stories, the owner of the Ferris Wheel had missed three inspections including one scheduled for the day of the accident. The owner, Bud Williams, was convicted of negligence and got some jail time.

The town wasn't held liable, but the family received two million dollars from the manufacturer of the Ferris Wheel because of a faulty design. All of the Ferris Wheels with the same design were ordered not to run until the defect was fixed, but the manufacturer didn't tell the companies.

I kept looking up Larry Eastburn. I found where he asked for a transfer with his company to Texas. Another story, this one only a month ago, told of the death of his wif., A year before, he lost a son in the war in Afghanistan.

I powered down my computer and went to bed. My last thought for the evening was, I could see how the man might lose it.

CHAPTER 49

My alarm went off at five-thirty a.m.

All of the killings took place after six-thirty in the evening, so I deemed it safe to go on a run. After that I made an appointment for Nutmeg at the groomers. Tonight the entire town would be out in force to watch the lighting of the Christmas tree and the official start of the Moonstone Lake Twenty-fifth Annual Festival of Lights.

Jess Morgan, the head of our CSI team assured Keith every killing took place from the top of a building. To assure the safety of the crowd, there would be an officer, either Highway Patrol, Catoosa County Sheriff, or Moonstone Police and our auxiliary on each building with binoculars and rifles with scopes.

My thinking ran along the line of everyone else's. We couldn't stop living, but the utmost care had to be taken to assure no one was injured.

I figured the killer worked somewhere and couldn't get to town and situated until after six. When I got back in from my morning errands, which included a shopping trip to Discount Groceries to restock my junk food shelves, I would do more research on Larry Eastburn.

Before it got too late in the afternoon, I wanted to check on Margie Steever and her crew. We really gave them the once over when Jackson Ramp was shot in their motel room.

After weeks of investigation, the addition of the other shootings, the trajectory of the bullet and searching the background of everyone in the group, it was decided they had nothing to do with Ramp's death.

Timothy Robin Clark, Skylar's father, had been transferred to a prison farm upstate where he would be held until his auto theft case came up for trial.

Keith had a long talk with Renee, Margie, Ashly and Anna. They all let out a deep breath at the thought of not having to look over their shoulders wondering what Tim would do next.

Demount's troubles began with an extortion ring and not with the children whose parents were approached and offered money to sully his reputation.

Tim Clark got the blame for Skylar's part in that also. Margie and Skylar had nothing to do with any of it. Tim tried to make them afraid in hopes Margie would go along with the plan to get money from the TV star.

Tim Clark was where he needed to be.

Chapter 50

"Arizona, what happened?" Someone pushed on my arm and tried to push my hair away from my face.

I tried to sit up but I couldn't. It would take more energy and concentration than I could muster. "I'm not sure. Where am I?" I could tell someone had my leg in the air. I looked down toward my feet as much as I could without lifting my head.

An EMT held my leg up with one hand under my heel and another midway up my leg below my knee. I recognized Jim Dudley. He did something to the top of my leg and I flinched.

I couldn't watch long. It took too much effort to raise my head the little bit I needed to in order to see. My head pounded. I closed my eyes. Someone shook my shoulder. "Ary, stay with me. We will have you on your way to the hospital in a minute.

First they need to stop the bleeding."

I wanted to raise my head again but my energy was spent. I closed my eyes to try to block out the pain in the back of my head and my thigh.

"Arizona. Can you tell me what happened? Anything?"

"Where is Nutmeg?" I could make out her shadowy figure as she crawled commando style toward me. She put her head on my belly and whined. "Is she hurt?" I looked up at Keith, who I now realized had been asking the questions. He knelt on both knees to get as close to me as he could.

"She is fine. The blood on her is yours. You were shot in the upper thigh. The wound is clean, it went in and out without hitting the bone or your femoral artery."

I closed my eyes again. The entire ordeal seemed to be way too much effort. I heard the EMT say to Keith, "You might as well give her a rest, Chief. The pain meds, along with the shock, I doubt you could believe anything she would tell you anyway. Let's get her to the hospital. There is a unit of blood waiting for her. It will help a great deal."

CHAPTER 51

I came to in a noisy place with blinding lights shining in my face. Many people talked at once, but I couldn't keep my mind on what each one said. I quit trying and closed my eyes again.

Someone fooled with my head, and another two or three people were down by my leg. I wanted them to be quiet and leave me alone.

Mother's voice broke through my fog. "Arizona, it's me, Mom. You have been hurt, but the doctors assure me you will be fine. Seems you were shot in the leg. When you fell, you hit your head on the concrete sidewalk in front of Discount Grocery.

"Do you remember any of those happenings?"

I tried to shake my head no but someone behind me said, "Lay still, Miss Summers. Only a few more stitches and I will be done. One day when you tell the story of today, you can add it took twelve stitches to close the gash on the back of your head."

I just wanted to go back to sleep.

Aunt Sandy's mellow voice filtered lightly through the fog. "Arizona, Ary, can you hear me? You need to stay awake. The doctors don't want you to go to sleep."

I squeezed her hand. I wanted to answer her, but it took too much effort. It took me forever to ask the question on my mind. "Where is my dog?"

Mom chuckled. "She is under the bed. She was going to bite anyone who would not let her in here including me, Sandra and Keith. Don't call her. If she comes out from under the bed they promise to throw her out, no matter what."

I opened my eyes in spite of the pounding in my head and leg. They were out of sync with each other. Head-pound, leg-pound, head-pound. I knew if it didn't stop I would throw up.

"Mom, where's Mom?"

"I'm right here dear." She took my hand.

I turned to her and said, "Mom, I've been shot."

The room got quiet. I had a feeling they already knew.

CHAPTER 52

"Look who's awake."

Mom sat by a bed. My bed, I guessed. I reached up and felt the back of my head. Someone had shaved a big chunk out of my hair. I couldn't put together what happened.

I looked around. The effort made me dizzy and I had to close my eyes again. "Am I in the hospital?"

"Yes, honey, since Friday. It is good to see you awake."

"Since Friday, what is today?"

"It is Sunday. You've slept mostly for the last three days. Do you feel any better?"

"Better than what? My head is pounding and my leg throbs. If I'm in the hospital, they could surely give me something for pain."

"They do, dear. The doctor assures us you will begin to improve once you begin to move around. Would you like to sit up?"

"No thanks. Could I have a drink of water?" Mom took a glass of ice off of a table near the bed and put a teaspoon of ice in my mouth. "If it is Sunday, I missed the Christmas tree lighting, the parade and the first day of the cooking contest."

I had more to say, but I needed to lay back and close my eyes.

She patted my arm. "You are fine, dear. The sniper shot you in the leg. It is quite a miracle since he hasn't missed before. Do you remember anything?"

"No, but I have a question. If I got shot in the leg, what is wrong with my head?'

"When they found you, you were lying with your head against a concrete lamppost. You have a pretty good gash back there."

"Where is Nutmeg? Where is my dog?"

"She is fine. She's with Keith. I think she likes being a police dog. The doctors let her come in at night and sleep under your bed."

"They do?"

CHAPTER 53

Aunt Sandy walked into the room. I looked up and she said, "Good, you're awake. We are supposed to call Keith as soon as you are able to talk. There are some wild stories going around town about you and this shooting. Do you feel like talking to him?"

"I guess, but I don't remember much. I was on my way…"

Sandy held up her hand to stop me. "Wait for Keith. No use telling your story twice, and I know from experience people remember more when someone asks them questions. I wouldn't know what questions to ask."

I didn't have enough energy to stay awake waiting for Keith so I closed my eyes.

"Arizona, it's time you sat up, get out of that bed and sit in a chair. I'll call someone to help you."

"Aunt Sandy, don't."

It was too late, a young man in a white uniform came to the doorway and asked, "What can I help you with?"

"She needs to sit in the chair."

He pulled a small black notebook out of his pocket and flipped a few pages. "You sure do, Miss Summers. There is a note here telling me to wake you up this evening and help you to a chair. The doctor would like you to sit in it for a half-an-hour."

With his help I put my legs over the edge of the bed. Talk about pain. Blood rushed to my head and pain ran down my leg. "Are you sure this is necessary?" I asked.

"You'll never get stronger, learn to walk on that leg or get out of here until you follow the steps. They are sit in a chair, go to the bathroom without help, walk around the floor for five minutes and eat an entire meal."

"That's a lot."

"No really," he said. "You used to do all of that within an hour before you got shot.

"Is it true you flew through the air and landed several feet away from where you first stood?"

"I don't remember anything like that, but if I had to guess, I'd say no."

Once I sat in the chair, he pulled out a footstool, put a pillow under my leg to relieve the pressure and tucked a blanket around me. "I'll be back in a little while to see how you're doing." He handed me the call button. "If you feel dizzy or sick, press this button."

I looked at his name tag. "Thanks Dakota."

It took a few minutes to catch my breath after

Dakota left the room. A lady from the cafeteria came in and sat a tray on my table and pulled it in front of me so I could eat. Under the cloche sat a bowl of peaches, orange Jello, luke-warm coffee, a bowl of chicken broth and a piece of white bread with a pad of frozen butter next to it. "I hope they don't consider this the entire meal I need to eat."

Aunt Sandy moved closer to take a look. "At least drink the broth and eat the Jello. I doubt the stuff they have been putting in your arm is too filling."

As I finished what I could, Keith came in. The grin on his face lit up the entire room. He walked straight up to me and kissed me on the lips. He didn't seem to care my aunt sat in a chair in the corner. "I take back all of the smart remarks I've made about calling you Detective Summers. This investigation isn't near as fun as the ones we have done together. How do you feel?"

"I'll put it to you this way. I only have one spot on my body that doesn't hurt." I touched my finger to the end of my nose. "Right there."

He leaned over and kissed it. "Sorry, I need to ask you these questions, but the way this is going, I don't know how long I have before something else happens."

"Ask away."

"Tell me what you remember."

"I took Nutmeg to the groomers and walked over to Discount Grocery. There was a lady in a red cape at the corner about three blocks away. I'd seen her several times and I remember I wanted to meet her so I sped up my pace and headed her way.

"I heard a loud noise. It sounded like a car backfired. Something hit my left shoulder. Next thing I know, I'm on the ground and EMT's are working on me."

He had a pen and pad in his hands but he didn't write anything down. "And that is it? The doctor said you have a nasty bruise on your shoulder, but you were not around anything to have made the mark. You were found at the bottom of a concrete lamppost at the edge of the street, near the curb. You were shot in your right leg. How do you account for the bruise on your left shoulder?"

"Honestly, Keith, I don't recall any more than I told you. I do remember I thought maybe a car hit me and knocked me down."

"There was no car. The street had barricades to keep traffic out. You were in a pedestrian-only zone.

"Four witnesses told me what happened. They all said nearly the same thing. I'll read you what Mary Christianson said... *it happened very fast. I waved at Arizona who was walking on the other side of Main Street. I just turned the corner at Second and Main so I was walking toward her. I heard a sound I thought to be a gunshot. Arizona flew through the air, I know a good three feet. She landed on the sidewalk. Her head bounced off the lamppost behind her...* He looked me in the eye. What do you think?"

I looked from Keith to my Aunt Sandy. "I don't know what to think. I told you what I saw and heard. I don't have anything else to add."

"Ok, Arizona, this is what Mayor James saw... *I*

was about ten paces behind Arizona when I heard what I thought to be a gunshot. I flattened myself on the brick behind me. Miss Summers flew about two or three feet and ended up at the bottom of a lamp post in front of the grocery store. At first I thought maybe the force of the bullet moved her, but she was shot in the right leg. I've played it over and over in my head.

It was as if a flying object ran into her at full speed and the impact threw her in the air. What I would picture getting hit by a car would look like. Only, there was no car...

He closed his notebook and looked at me. "There are two more accounts, one from Johnny Kake and another from Doris Sims. They all say the same thing without much variation. And I talked to all of them separately before they had a chance to talk to one another."

Tears welled up in my eyes. I tried to hold them back. "I can't explain it. Maybe it wasn't my time to go. Whatever it was, I am thankful for it. The sniper has never missed before. I'm one lucky lady."

"Yes you are," Aunt Sandy and Keith said at the same time.

We sat in silence.

CHAPTER 54

I didn't get to go home for another day. Physical therapy came in and showed me how to walk with a cane.

Mom asked if I wanted to stay with her so I didn't have any steps, but I wanted to be alone. All the talk about me flying through the air, a sniper shooting at me and not being able to pet Nutmeg made me want to scream.

Keith helped me to my apartment and Lewis came up personally to bring my favorite meal, shrimp scampi, Caesar salad and a baked potato with sour cream and lots of butter. I sat on the couch with pillows piled up on the arm and my feet off the floor. Nutmeg whined a little because she had to lie on the floor, but she recovered quickly.

Lewis leaned over, kissed the top of my head and said, "I've missed you. How do you feel?"

"Much better. My leg doesn't hurt near as bad as my head. Doctor said when I get the stitches out it will be better. Three more days. How's the cooking contest?"

"Your Aunt Sandy and I are doing a bang up job if I must say so myself. Tammy Smith won best appetizer with stuffed mushrooms, Brent Long had best soup with a cold pumpkin creation.

"Best salad was won by Dannielle Walker. Tonight is best one-pot main dish. I hope you can, at least, come and watch."

"Oh, I plan to. Randy Malone is coming by to help me down the stairs, and Sandy said she has a chair for me and a footstool for my leg."

Keith said, "I was supposed to judge the appetizer round and then tonight the main dish, but I turned it over to Amy. With all the shootings, I didn't want to have to leave and ruin your event.

"There have been no more shootings since you were wounded. I'm not sure why. By the way, Jess Morgan will be by to take Nutmeg for a run tonight. I've been running with her in the morning and Jess in the evening."

"That is a lot to ask," I said,

He stepped closer and took my hand. "Jess has one of those baby running carriages and his boy loves it. He's been picking Nutmeg up in his van and they go all the way to the north side to city park to run. Nothing going on over there, and we deem it pretty safe."

Lewis, who had sat on the edge of a chair said, "I need to get back. See you later, Arizona, glad you are home."

Keith left. We were alone at last. I ate every bite of the plate Lewis brought, and Nutmeg ate all the food Keith fed her. I fell asleep on the couch.

A sharp knock woke me up. I hobbled to the door to let Randy in. "Is it time already?"

"Sure is. I don't want to hurt your feelings, but you need to do a little work on yourself before we head down to the restaurant."

"That bad?"

He looked at Nutmeg who barked once. "That bad," he said.

"How much time do I have to get ready?"

"I'll take Nutmeg for a walk and be back in about fifteen minutes."

They left. When I saw myself in the bathroom mirror, I realized how tactful Randy had been.

The evening turned out to be what I needed. Everyone in the place wished me well. The atmosphere was sparkly and happy. Millie Drake won best pot meal.

By the time I got back to my apartment, I knew I needed to go to bed. I said to Randy, "Tell me something. Since in order to get up here to my apartment, a person has to either come in through a door in the restaurant, which needs a four number code, or the front which needs a different code. Does that mean everyone has the codes to come and go as they please?"

"Not really. Keith has the locksmith change them every night at ten. Only the people who live here have the code. The next day, Keith gives it out as needed and they change it again at ten p.m.

"It is a hassle, but you are safe."

CHAPTER 55

The bandage on my leg had some sort of plastic wrapping on it. As badly as I wanted to soak in a hot tub. I couldn't, so I took a shower.

It wore me out. I put on a sleep shirt, a pair of shorts and went to bed. I heard Jess come get Nutmeg, and I kind of remember when she came back in.

I woke with a start. A gentle breeze brushed against my cheek. Nutmeg whined, jumped off the bed and crawled under it. She didn't bark.

Fear rose in my throat, heat took over my body and I could hardly catch my breath.

Someone said in a soft, mellow voice, "Mary Beth, don't be afraid, it is me, your mother."

I sat up. "Mary Beth? My mother? Impossible."

I got out of bed, took a pillow with me as a security blanket. I held it to my chest and hugged it as hard as I could. I backed away, and if I could have, I would have hidden in my closet or joined my dog under the bed. I opened my eyes.

The Lady in Red sat in my bedroom chair with her hands crossed in her lap. I couldn't see her feet.

"My name is Arizona Summers. My mother came and got me from an orphanage in Phoenix. My mother is Emma Summers," I said.

She reached out her hand and touched my arm. I could see right through it. Couldn't be. "Who are you, really?"

"Relax, Mary Beth, and let me explain."

"Please don't call me Mary Beth."

"All right, Arizona. Please let me tell you what I came here to say. I had a special dispensation from my Angel to stay down here a year and observe you. When the man tried to kill you last week, I stepped in. I knew better than to interfere with the human world, but I couldn't let him kill you."

"So when witnesses said I flew through the air, it was you who pushed me?"

"I'm sorry, my love, I didn't mean to push you so hard. I didn't know what strength I had. I've never been dead before."

"Give me a break. This is too fantastic to comprehend. Are you telling me you died and an Angel let you come to earth and visit me?"

"Correct. But I broke the rules. There weren't many, don't interact with anyone, don't change the course of human life and come when I'm called."

"That's why no one else saw you. Why sometimes you were in my photographs and sometimes not? Why when I tried to catch up with you to see you closer, you disappeared?"

"Exactly, my love. Please let me explain to you what happened to me. I have very little time left here on earth. I only hope I get to stay long enough to tell you what I want to tell you."

I couldn't help myself. I believed her and doubted my own sanity at the same time. "Do you want some tea?"

She smiled, her face turned radiant. "I don't eat or drink anymore. I just am. Don't get me wrong. I'm not sad or unhappy. I had one wish and Geraldine, my Angel, granted it.

"Let me talk and you listen."

I shook my head yes. Nutmeg stirred under the bed but didn't come out.

"I was a teenager when your father came to town. He swept me off my feet, and I left a loving home to go with him.

"I can't judge whether he was a bad man or not. It is not for me to say, nor am I allowed to. He killed some people and was sent to prison.

"His family had the same outlook as he did. I promised myself I would not let them have you. I hid you at the orphanage with the plan of picking you up again once I got settled.

"I can't make excuses. I have learned since I have been in this form, I, and I, alone was responsible for every decision I ever made.

"Life got in the way. I am not allowed to tell you about it. It would only sound like excuses. When I managed to get back, you were gone. A lady came from another state and took you away. She changed your name and gave you a wonderful life.

"I never knew what happened to you until a few months ago when I left my mortal life. I wanted to come and tell you only one thing. I thought about you EVERY day of my life. I never stopped loving you or praying you were okay and living a good life."

She sat and stared at me.

"I must go now. I lost my time with you by moving you out of the way of that bullet, but I would do it all again. I love you, I always have.

"There are angels looking after you and I will be one of them. I won't see you again or be able to come to you, but I hope you will always remember I am there."

She handed me a fine silver chain with a butterfly dangling from it. "Take this. Keep it close to your heart to remind you that you have been lucky twice. I have always loved you and so does Emma. Many people don't even have one person to count on."

She leaned forward and kissed me on the forehead. I felt as if a cool breeze touched me, like before.

"May I ask for one thing before you go?"

"Yes, I will grant your wish if it is within my power."

"Please take off your hood and let me see your face. I never want to forget it or this moment in time."

She smiled and it lit the area surrounding her face. She turned slowly from side to side and then she was gone.

I didn't think it could have been real. I didn't

believe in Angels. I didn't know anything about them. Religion had never been a big part of my life.

I fell asleep. The bed moved slightly when Nutmeg came back to bed.

When I woke in the morning, I didn't want to wake up. It was the most beautiful dream I'd ever had. I closed my eyes and tried to conjure it up one more time.

I turned over on my side and something lay beside me. I picked it up. In my hand I held a fine silver chain with a delicate filigree butterfly dangling from a loop attached to it.

I tried to slip the chain over my head but it wasn't long enough. I opened the clasp and fastened it again around my neck. The butterfly sparkled in the morning sun.

I knew then it was true. Every word, every whisper, every gentle breeze as it touched my face had been an angel, my mother.

CHAPTER 56

I didn't work Thursday, but I did go down and take part in the cooking contest as I should have all along.

My first surprise, Mom, Johnny, Riley and Margie sat in the front row. Margie Gold's grandson entered the dessert portion of the contest. He had to have given them passes to get in. They all smiled and waved.

The desserts were fabulous. My favorites were Molten Chocolate Crackle Pie, Salted Caramel Tarts, Brown Butter Rum Cannoli and Pumpkin Cream Cheese Swirl Bars.

Even though the judges were not supposed to know who made which dessert, each section where the chef sat with his guests tensed up as their dessert went before the judges.

At the end of the evening the winners were

announced. All the desserts were cut and served to the guests. It almost made one forget about the horror in Moonstone Lake for the last weeks.

Before Mother left, I went to sit with her and her friends. Seems Margie's grandson, Michael, had a real knack for cooking. They all beamed at him as they devoured his dish.

Aunt Sandy came by, and the first thing she did was notice my butterfly pendant and ask me where I got it.

At the same time, my mom gave me the strangest look. She didn't seem to be able to take her eyes off of the necklace.

"I'm not sure. It was in one of my desk drawers near the back. I had to do some heavy cleaning on it to be able to wear it. I most likely bought it when I went to garage sales every Saturday morning."

"Well, it is beautiful."

"Thanks."

Mom still looked intently at my neck. "Are you okay?" I asked.

"I had a friend many years ago who had a necklace just like it. I hadn't thought about it for years. It's exquisite, dear, it fits you." She smiled and looked away.

Jess came in about nine with his boy. They had a little dessert and took Nutmeg with them for an evening run.

Since I'd been shot, I'd hardly seen Keith. He had his hands full with the families of the victims and following leads to try to catch the madman who killed our townspeople.

I bowed out early. I had most of my strength

back, but I still needed my rest.

After the stitches came out on Saturday, I knew I would feel one hundred percent better.

I'd been home about an hour when there was a knock at my door. It was Mother.

"Hi, Mom, it's rare for you to come up here. Are you okay?"

"Yes, I wanted to have another look at your pendant."

My stomach leaped to my throat. I knew I could never tell anyone about my encounter with an apparition of my birth mother. Not only would no one believe it, but it was the most deep and personal event of my life. To repeat it would be, well, unconscionable. "Please, come in. Have time for some tea?"

"No, I'm fine. I wondered if you would be up this late."

"Since I was injured, Jess Morgan and his son have come every night to take Nutmeg for a run."

"How sweet. Aren't you afraid for their safety?"

"I was until I found out they take her over to the other side of town, way out of the Festival area. Hopefully, I will at least be able to walk her in a day or two."

She leaned close to me. "About the butterfly, dear. I want to tell you a story."

I hoped I looked calm and unsurprised, because I sure didn't feel like it inside. "Sure. I noticed how you looked at it downstairs."

"Remember when I told you I went to culinary school with your real grandmother? While we were there, we went to an estate sale. Jo Ann, your grandmother, bid on a necklace like the one you are wearing. She said it was for your mother, Angela. She said she would put it back for a special occasion.

"If you look at the picture of your mother I gave you, you will see she had it on. The only way this story could be any better is if your mother herself had been able to give it to you."

My emotions played ping pong in my stomach and I did my best to hide the tears I knew were coming at any minute.

Thank goodness Jess opened the door and Nutmeg came bounding in. She ran straight to Mom and wagged her tail waiting to be petted.

Mom obliged her and then stood. "You look tired, dear. You've had a long day. I wanted to tell you how miraculous it is you found that necklace. You should cherish it. I only know of one other in existence."

I walked her to the door and gave her a hug. "I love you, Mom."

"I love you too, Arizona."

CHAPTER 57

My phone rang at eleven-thirty, a picture of Keith flashed onto the screen. "Hi, hope I didn't wake you. I drove by and saw your light on. I thought I'd take a chance."

"No, I'm up. Where are you?"

"Truthfully, I'm sitting in my cruiser outside."

"You can come up if you like."

"Sure, I am beginning to forget what you look like. It has been a long time since I got to sit and talk with you."

I laughed. "It isn't that bad. Let yourself in. I don't do stairs yet." While I waited for him to come in, I put on a light-weight robe.

When the door opened, he stuck his head in and said, "I'm here."

I met him half way. He took me in his arms and held me for a long moment. "You feel so good. I hear you were part of the cooking contest tonight. I figured you would be worn out and already asleep."

We sat together on the couch. "Want something to drink?"

"Is there anything to eat up here?"

"Yes. Lewis has kept the fridge stocked since I got out of the hospital. Do you want a sandwich or something hot?"

He got up and went to the kitchen. "I'll look for myself.

"I'm going for this casserole." He held it up to his face and said, "I smell cheese, chicken and stuffing." He proceeded to take a plate from the cabinet, dished himself a hearty helping and put it in the microwave.

I fixed us both a cup of raspberry lemon zinger tea, and when he sat at the table to eat, I sat with him.

"Any progress on the identity of our shooter?"

His brow wrinkled as he looked up at me. "No. It's driving me crazy. There hasn't been any more trouble since he shot you, but then I have at least three men on the roofs at all times. I need to catch him. We can't sustain a budget for all the extra help for too long. But it is better than another killing."

"Since you didn't ask me why I'm up so late, I'll tell you anyway. This all began with Jackson Ramp. He was shot in a motel room, through an open door. Jess said the trajectory of the bullet showed the shooter to be on the same plane as the victim.

"All the other shootings were done from a rooftop or maybe from a tree top. The only thing they have in common with Ramp is they were all killed with a .243."

He finished his food, rinsed his plate out in the sink and put it in the dishwasher. Instead of sitting back in a kitchen chair, he took my hand and led me to the couch. Once we were settled, he said, "Go on."

"Maybe they all meant something to him. Maybe the killings are not random at all."

"It is possible, but I don't see how, especially you."

"Maybe I wasn't the target. I could be alive because he realized I wasn't the target."

He put his arm around me and pulled me close. "We can begin to look into it in the morning. Right now, I couldn't keep my mind on it. I'm much too tired."

I walked him to the door and when he kissed me goodnight, his energy seemed to come back. One thing might have led to another, but his cell phone rang. "You're kidding me," he said. He took a deep breath and shook his head. "Randy needs help. There is a fight at the Beer Garden. I need to go before someone gets hurt. I'll see you tomorrow. Are you going to work?"

"I am. It'll be my first full day. Come by when you have time. Meanwhile, I'll take my computer and begin a search to see if I can tie these people together."

CHAPTER 58

The place buzzed all morning with the anticipation of the announcement of the winners of the cooking contest later in the evening.

Several times I went back to check with Lewis to make sure I had all my ducks in a row as to how we would present the awards. We thought it best to do the first place in each category and then go back with the second and third place winners.

It didn't take long for us to decide to announce all three winners of each category at the same time. It would keep the suspense going throughout the evening.

The secretary of the Chamber of Commerce happened to be a calligraphy expert and did the awards for nearly every event in town, including the high school graduations and marriage licenses.

They all lay face down on the tabletop of my

booth, each in a separate sealed envelope. I did my best to recruit Lewis to announce the winners. The man carried himself in a regal manner, not to mention the fact he happened to be the best looking man of his age I knew.

He said no. He and his wife wanted to watch the gala. I ended up with the job.

By noon, I had the certificates in order and the checks written for all three spots in all the contests.

I hoped I had nothing to do until four when I went up to change for the celebration.

The one thing I didn't tell Keith; I intended to try to tie each murdered person to Larry Eastburn. In my heart, I knew he was the key to the entire ordeal.

Jackson Ramp, Private investigator. I called the records keeper at the police station and asked, "Denise, do you still have the client list from the reports Keith confiscated from Ramp's office?"

"Sure, they are in the master file in Keith's office. Do you need them?"

"Yes and no. What I need is to see if Jackson Ramp had a client by the name of Larry Eastburn, or maybe Bud Williams (the owner of the Ferris Wheel). It would have been about twenty years ago."

"I'm the one who went through the appointment books when they came in. Ramp turned fifty a week before he died. I don't have time to go over them again now, but if you can come get them, I can sign them out to you for the day. They need to be back here tonight, though.

"There is a chain of custody that can't be broken when we are building a murder case."

"Can you seal them in an envelope, and I'll send someone for them. I'll have them back in a few hours."

She agreed and we hung up.

CHAPTER 59

About twenty minutes later Keith came in carrying the file I'd asked for. He sat it on the table in front of my computer. "Sorry, I can't let this out of police custody. Think you could find what you are looking for while I have lunch?"

"I'll make sure I do," I said. "What are you hungry for?"

"I heard there was a limited menu today because of the awards banquet tonight. If a burger is on the menu, I'll take that."

He gave his order to the waitress when she came by to see if he wanted coffee. He declined in favor of a strawberry milkshake. He nodded toward the envelope I'd opened. "Do you know what you're looking for there?"

"No, but if I see it, I'll know."

We sat in silence, me with my nose into the

calendars from twenty years ago and Keith waiting for his lunch. I found it, January 16, 2002, Bud (Walter) Williams hired Jackson Ramp to follow Larry Eastburn. The reason in the P.I.'s notes read, Williams thinks Eastburn is out to get him. Wants surveillance on his house and himself to keep Eastburn from hurting him or his family.

A notation referred me to three years later when Bud Williams was tried and convicted in a wrongful death suit filed by Eastburn in regard to his son. Bud Williams had been in jail about six months by then and had over nine years left on his sentence for negligence of the operation of the Ferris Wheel. Eastburn received a judgement of two million dollars against Williams. I doubt he ever paid the money.

I needed to see what happened to Williams once he finished his prison sentence. I took copious notes.

By the time Keith finished his lunch, I had found all the information I needed. I put the contents the way I found them and pushed the envelope back to Keith.

"So what did you find?"

I put my hand on his. "I'm not ready to share my information yet. I don't have what I need. Are you going to be able to come to the awards tonight?"

"I'm going to try my best. I'd better go now. Thanks for lunch. I'll try to see you this evening."

In compliance with my doctor's orders, I got off my bench and walked around. One more day and the stitches would be out of my leg and my head. A long hot bath never sounded so good.

Aunt Sandy sat on a lounge chair next to her work station. The café had hardly any customers. I wanted to ask her what she was reading but I knew if I did, the book club would come up so I skipped my question.

"Look who's up and around," she said. "How are you? Looks like you have the cane mastered."

Nutmeg came out from under the podium where she slept, as soon as she heard my voice.

Aunt Sandy stood and walked toward us. "I don't know if dogs can be sleep deprived, but Nutmeg hasn't had much of a nap today. The Monroe girls and their folks were here for an early breakfast, and the three little ones crawled under the table and petted her. Keith took her outside for a walk after lunch. That is one spoiled dog."

I reached down and petted her. "She deserves it. I would take her for a walk but since she just came back, I'll pass.

"I'm about ready to go upstairs, rest a little and get ready for tonight. How about you?"

She laughed. "Get your stuff and I'll go now, just to make sure you don't fall down the stairs."

CHAPTER 60

I knew I needed to rest my leg and take a couple of Tyleno,l but I had one thing I wanted to do first.

I got a red marker, a black marker and a piece of poster paper from the spare bedroom. In the center I drew a large circle with my black marker. Inside the circle in red ink I printed, Larry Eastburn. I made a dozen smaller circles around it and said a silent prayer I wouldn't need that many. I drew a line from each small circle to my one bigger one.

I made a smaller oval outside my big round of circles. In the small one I wrote Bud Williams but instead of connecting it to Eastburn, I put Jackson Ramp in one and connected one end to Eastburn and the other to Williams.

I put my name in a circle, but I didn't make a line. I wasn't completely sure he meant to shoot me. Lady in Red or not, if he wanted to kill me, I think he would have.

I lay on my bed but first I set an alarm. Since I got hurt, I couldn't rely on myself to get up when I needed to.

I left myself an hour to shower and dress for the affair downstairs. I waited until fifteen minutes before we were to go downstairs and took the Tylenol, hoping it would kick in and last all evening.

None of my pants would fit over my swollen leg. I'd been wearing sweat pants all week but it wouldn't work for tonight so I chose a skirt and vest. I wore a white long-sleeve blouse under a royal blue and black checkered vest and a royal blue skirt. I took the time to French braid my hair and put on a little eye liner and mascara.

Before we left the apartment, I checked myself in the mirror. The butterfly sparkled in the light.

My goal was to get downstairs early and put Nutmeg in the overflow dining room behind the contestants. She wouldn't make a sound, and I didn't want her to be out front alone.

Benny had a table set up for me off to the side of the winners' chairs. They didn't know they were winners and would stay in the audience until, if and when, their names were called.

Exactly at the stroke of five, I stood and quieted the crowd. "I want to welcome you to the First Annual Festival of Lights Cooking Contest. We have had great participation. Without further ado, we will start the awards ceremony.

"We will begin with the third place winner of the appetizer round..."

(THE WINNING RECIPES ARE AT THE END OF THE BOOK)

It went like that from the appetizer round and continued all the way to the winners of the dessert round.

As the winners received their certificates and monetary prizes, they moved to the section we had roped off for them to sit.

"I know some of you have been here every evening for seven days, so we are going to adjourn this early. Don't forget, the thirty-six winners will be the guests of Moonstone Café and Sunday Brunch tomorrow afternoon for dinner. We will begin seating at five-thirty, and appetizers will be served at six.

"The menu will be the first place winners' recipes prepared by our Chef Lewis Davis and his crew.

"We will see the winners then. Please pick up your souvenir from this year's contest on your way out. Thank you all for coming. Have a safe trip home."

Keith came up behind me and put a hand on each of my shoulders. He leaned close to my neck and said, "I think you missed your calling. You did a great job. Everyone here left smiling."

CHAPTER 61

Lewis fixed Nutmeg a plate of his famous homemade dog food and me a ribeye steak, baked potato, and a Caesar salad. He plated up the same thing for himself and sat at the counter across from me to eat. "I'll be glad when the sniper is caught. No one has been killed since you were shot six days ago. The entire town is tense. I can feel it all day, every day."

I cut my steak and put two more helpings of sour cream on my potato. "Do you remember, it would have been when you first began working here, a boy fell off a Ferris Wheel and died?"

"Yes, it is one of those things you never forget. What made it worse was your Aunt Sandra happened to be on the ride at the same time, almost directly across from the boy and saw the entire thing.

"It was a horrid ordeal for the family of the boy, the witnesses, the town and almost put an end to our Festival of Lights."

I took a few bites of my dinner. I didn't want him to think the only reason I had dinner with him was to pick his brain. "Why did we have a Ferris Wheel in the first place?"

"The owner of the ride had a brother in town. He recommended his brother who took the wheel all over the country. The ride and the games they brought to town were popular. At the city council meeting right before the accident, they had actually voted to expand the area the next year and add a Tilt-a-Whirl."

"Do you remember the man's brother's name?"

He stood and took my plate. "How about a piece of raspberry cobbler with ice cream? I don't recall his name. I do remember he delivered milk and lived over near the kid and his parents.

"The boy's father harassed him so much, he moved to Centerville. The story was that Larry Eastburn, the father of the boy who was fatally wounded, blamed the brother. He said no one would have thought to add part of a carnival to our celebration had it not been for him. Right now, his name escapes me.

"I remember it was an unusual first name. Shane or Sean or something like that."

"Seth," I said.

"Yes, Seth."

"Lewis, one of the victims of this sniper was Seth Williams. Did you know Larry Eastburn, Sr.?"

"I knew both Larry Eastburns, the one before his

son's death and one after. Believe me, they were nothing alike. We weren't friends, but he said hi when he saw me. He seemed to be a pleasant fellow.

"After the boy's accident, he was hell on wheels. He picked fights everywhere he went and held a grudge against most of the townsfolk. His wife couldn't take living here. She had to go past the place the Ferris Wheel sat, on her way to and from work.

"About six months after the accident, they moved. I don't know where. The entire town hated what happened to his boy. He would never accept that it was a tragic accident."

I wanted to help him clean up, but he wouldn't hear of it. On my way out I said, "I guess you don't know the names of the people killed by the sniper?"

"Just know you were wounded. To tell you the truth, I don't watch the news except for the weather. My wife and daughter keep me in the loop. I bet I haven't watched a TV show in ten years. When I leave here, I am ready to read and listen to music and enjoy my family. I guess I'm weird."

I walked over and kissed him on the cheek. "Thanks for dinner." When I got to the door I turned around and said, "You're not weird, you're wonderful."

Jesse couldn't come to take Nutmeg for a walk so I sat on the front stoop and watched her run around. When she came back, she seemed perfectly happy and didn't act like she missed Jess.

I navigated the stairs easily. Between the handrail and the cane, I had become an expert.

Once in my apartment, I slipped on some pajamas and went into the living room where I'd fastened my murder board on the wall with thumbtacks.

In one of the circles I wrote Seth Williams and drew a line straight to Larry Eastburn.

I connected Jackson Ramp, Bud Williams, Seth Williams and Ronny Watts to Larry Eastburn. What on earth could a middle-aged crafter from Wisconsin, Arlene Mann, have to do with the death of Larry's son?

Arlene Mann didn't have many entries on Google. She lived in Madison with her husband. She had three grown boys. She made Toffee with dark chocolate ganache. She had been to the festival since the very first year.

I needed to place her somewhere around Larry or his son. I found what I sought in the transcripts of the wrongful death suit.

Arlene Mann, one of twenty-one witnesses who were either on the ride or close enough to see what happened. She testified for the defense. In her testimony she said…*The young man tried to spin the car completely over. He rocked back and forth time and time again, like someone trying to gather height with a swing.* Defense Attorney- *Where were you when you saw the boy try to tip the car he rode in?* Arlene Mann- *I sat right below him. I looked up because the girl in the seat with him screamed over and over for the boy to stop.* Defense Attorney- *Did the boy stop?* Arlene Mann- *No, he kept up the swaying. He even put his foot on the safety rail and stood to try to make the seat spin completely over.*

Prosecutor – *Why do you think you and only one other witness saw the boy stand in the car?* Arlene Mann- *I don't know, but I am telling you what I saw. I didn't take my eyes off of the boy because I thought he might fall on top of me. Maybe the others didn't have the same point of view as we did.*

I had all the information I needed on Mrs. Mann. I needed to know who the other witness who saw the boy jumping up and down in the seat was. If he or she lived in Moonstone Lake, I had a bad feeling they wouldn't be alive long.

I read the transcript until I waded through the testimony of all the people who saw the boy on the Ferris Wheel, New Year's Eve, 2001.

My stomach began to do flips, my hands began to sweat and the room darkened around me when I came upon the testimony of the other witness who saw Larry, Jr. rock the seat on the Ferris Wheel trying to make it go completely around the bar above it.

Aunt Sandy.

After I added Arlene Mann to my murder board, I only had one more question. Where was Larry Eastburn, Sr. now?

In my heart, I knew he would kill my Aunt Sandy if I didn't protect her.

I reached for my phone. It was one-forty-five in the morning. Keith might have finally had a chance to get some sleep. I'd present my findings to him first thing in the morning.

CHAPTER 62

I tossed and turned so much the rest of the night, Nutmeg jumped out of bed and slept on the floor.

Every five minutes I glanced over toward the clock on my bedside table hoping enough time passed so I could call Keith. The night dragged on.

I don't know what time I went to sleep, only that when the alarm sounded, I jumped out of bed and ran to the shower.

At seven a.m. I called Keith. "My, you sound chipper," he said.

"I do? Keith, I need to see you right away. I know who the sniper is, why he is killing and how all of the victims fit together. I also know who his next target is."

"Ary, slow down. How did you find out so much information in one day?"

"Keith, don't question me, come over here now.

I need to show you what I have. The next person on the killer's list is my Aunt Sandy. We need to stop it."

"Okay, I'll be right there."

I had a chill from standing around with only my undies on while I talked to Keith. I put on a pair of green sweat pants two sizes too big for me. My appointment to get my stitches removed was at nine. I wanted to be comfortable. I matched it with a white Moonstone Lake sweatshirt with the printing in red.

I looked like a Christmas tree, but I didn't care.

Keith pushed the downstairs buzzer and said, "I'm on my way up, don't shoot."

He was trying to be funny, but I was on edge and glad he called before he came through my door. He came up to me and took me in his arms. He held me a long moment until I said, "I have coffee ready."

He started toward the kitchen until I went toward the living room and told him, "It's in here."

The murder board loomed out from the pale green wall. "What's this?"

I handed him a mug of coffee. "It's my murder board."

"Yes," he said, "but who is Larry Eastburn? And why do you have him down as the sniper?"

"It's a long story, but I will condense it as much as possible."

Instead of sitting, he walked close to the board and looked at it intently. "Please, don't leave out anything. We at the police department have never heard of this man."

"Want me to warm your coffee?" I asked.

He shook his head no, reached into his shirt pocket, retrieved his notebook and pen and sat on the edge of the couch.

"Larry Eastman lived in Moonstone Lake for years. Twenty-years ago, his eighteen year old son fell to his death from a Ferris Wheel we had on the grounds.

"He hated the entire town and blamed most everyone in it for the death of his son. He filed a lawsuit against the city for allowing the carnival ride here in the first place. He sued the Mayor, the City Council, Bud (Walter) Williams, who owned the wheel, and anyone else who came near him, for wrongful death.

"He made it impossible for his wife and family to stay here. Five months after the accident, they moved across country and no one heard from him again. Mom said the outcome of all the lawsuits were published in the papers both here and in Stanfield and St. Louis.

"Bud Williams was sentenced to ten years for failing to inspect the ride and keep it up to code. Eastburn was awarded two million dollars in his wrongful death suit against Williams."

Keith got up to get more coffee, and I sat in my chair and waited. "So what makes you think he is a killer now, after twenty-years?"

"Because several things happened to Mr. Eastburn within the duration of a few months, and I fully believe he lost his mind.

"One of his son's was killed in Afghanistan and two months after that his wife died. My guess is he began to look at his life and decided to settle some scores.

"Here's how I have it figured. Bud Williams hired Jackson Ramp all those years ago to protect him from Eastburn. Eastburn and Ramp had several altercations. I think Larry Eastburn killed Ramp.

"Ronny Watts defended Bud Williams at his trial. Arlene Mann testified Larry Jr., at the time he fell from the ride, was attempting to swing the car higher and higher to make it swing completely over the top bar.

"Seth Williams lived near the Eastburns and suggested the town hire Bud to bring his Ferris Wheel and about twenty carnival games to the festival every year. The accident happened the last night of the fifth festival."

He turned away from the murder board and toward me. "What does your aunt have to do with all of this?"

I took a deep breath to try to steady my voice. "Aunt Sandy was the only other witness who saw the boy try to tip the car before a pin sheared off and one side of the seat fell causing the boy to slide off to his death.

"A girl who rode with Larry Jr. held on, and a man climbed the rigging and saved her."

"That is quite a story. Do you know where Mr. Eastburn is now?"

"No. And I haven't said anything to anyone about what I think I know."

He reached down to pull his cell phone from his pocket. "Randy, come over to the Moonstone Café. I need for you to guard Arizona's Aunt Sandy.

"I'll explain it all when you get here. I'll meet

you in the dining room.

"Before you come, run a check on a Larry Eastburn, Sr. I don't know what state he lives in or much about him."

"Isn't he the guy whose kid fell off a Ferris Wheel when we were kids?"

"Yes, Randy, one and the same. Try to find out what kind of car he drives, ask Denise to run a complete background check on him. I'll tell you everything else when I see you."

CHAPTER 63

My heart pounded as I realized Keith believed my entire scenario, but I had a problem. The gala for the winners of the cooking contest began at five. If I didn't start preparations now, it would be too late.

"Keith, as much as I want to be a part of all of this, I need to get downstairs and help with tonight's celebration. If you find anything out, please let me know. A simple phone call will be good enough."

He kissed me. "Arizona Summers, you will be the best detective I have. I only have one question. What sent you on this trail? Twenty years is a long time to hold a grudge."

"I couldn't put Jackson Ramp together with the rest of the victims. The way he was killed. The only clue to bring them all together was they were all shot with a .243.

"Mom has a picture in her room of a Ferris

Wheel with my Aunt Sandy riding in one of the cars. I bet I've looked at the picture hundreds of times. This time I saw several landmarks I recognized. I asked her why we no longer had a carnival ride.

"She relayed the story of the boy falling to his death and how his father almost single-handedly brought an end to the festival. Then there was the crap about Daniel Demount and the children. It didn't make sense to me. If he had been a threat to kids, the network would have gotten rid of him after the first incident.

"It had to be a money thing. Why else would it continue, and why else would the producer let him have a kid's program? I realized it had nothing to do with Skylar Steever or Timothy Clark. After that it was a natural progression of clues.

"I have to go. So many people have put so much time and effort into this event tonight. With my injury, I haven't even been around enough to know what some of the recipes are.

"In ten minutes I need to be at the hospital to have my stitches removed."

He opened the door and stood to the side of it. "Come on, grab a jacket and I'll take you. There is no faster way to travel than in a police cruiser."

CHAPTER 64

When I arrived at the kitchen, an hour later, I walked into a madhouse. All of our staff were called in for the day. Some were decorating tables, others put place settings out, and still others placed placards at each table so the winners would know where to sit.

"Hi Lewis, I'm ashamed to say this, but I don't know which appetizer won first place or the soup, salad or main dish. Can you help me out? I need to type up the recipes for Liz."

"I don't think you could help it, Ary. You can sit here with me and we will go over the finer details of tonight.

"The winner of the appetizer round is a Creamy cheese and Prosciutto cracker. I have them ready in the back if you would like to taste one. We are serving four per person."

They were delicious. I devoured six.

"Next, we have the soup, it is also ready. The winner was cold cucumber. I must tell you I was shocked when the judges picked a cold soup in the winter, but they did. The recipes we are sending home with tonight's guests, and Liz is highlighting in the paper, are in much smaller quantities than what I have used here."

"I wish I was eating dinner with them, but I am going to mix and mingle."

The soup was to die for.

"Okay, Jose and Donny are working on the salads now. The main dish is Tuscan Chicken Mac and Cheese. Sorry you can't taste it. We won't begin to make it until after five. It needs to be served right away.

"The dessert judges picked Chocolate Cheesecake Bars. The line cooks are working on them now. All in all it is some delicious food. I'm not sure it is a cohesive meal, but it is eclectic for sure. I forgot, the best salad is Cran-apple Bleu Cheese.

"Here is one copy of each recipe with the name of the winner under the name of the dish. We need thirty-six for the contestants, a few for the newspaper, and if it were me, I'd make about a hundred to put on the front counter. It will make the diners feel more involved.

"I commend you for closing all day today. I'm not sure we could have pulled off all this food and still fed the masses. By the way, I'd like to bring my wife for dinner tonight. She deserves it for putting up with all of my late nights lately."

"Sure, I always love to see her. I'd better get over to the library. They said they would print everything I need if I furnish the paper."

"Before you go, Ary, how's the leg?"

"It's one hundred percent better than before the stitches were removed. Thanks, Lewis. I don't think we could have pulled this contest together without your superior talents."

He raised his hand to shoo me off. "Flattery will get you everywhere."

CHAPTER 65

I went to the front of the restaurant to talk to Aunt Sandy. Instead I found Sally at the desk cleaning and dusting for the party. "Where's Sandy?"

Sally looked up at me from dusting the bottom of the display case. "She left. Officer Malloy from the police department escorted her out of here about an hour ago."

"Did he say where he was taking her?"

Sally stopped her chore, came closer to me and lowered her voice. "I only heard parts of the conversation. Something about the sniper and your aunt being in danger. Then I heard him say he wanted to keep her safe until they found the man.

"I got the feeling he knew who the killer was. When he told her the name of the man they were looking for, she turned pale, got her coat, and asked me to take over for her. Then she looked at the officer and said, '*I will be back here for the party tonight*'."

Nutmeg came out and stood beside me. "Want to go to the library with me?"

She turned around in circles and barked.

The town bustled. The festival was in full swing. Several times I had to turn sideways to get down the sidewalk because of all of the people.

I looked up and saw several men on rooftops. The crowd didn't seem to notice. People had armloads of packages or sat at tables outside the food trucks and ate.

The entire town vibrated with joy and laughter.

I'd still had no word from Keith.

No one occupied the library. I didn't expect them to. Janice Babcock, the main librarian, stood at the door when I went in. "It is difficult to be in here today. The sun is shining, people are smiling and happy and I'm stuck in here until five. Doesn't seem right. No one has been in here in days."

I smiled. "I have a job for you which might eat up some of your time."

She walked back toward the copier and took the ream of paper I carried out of my hand and laid it on the cabinet near her work station. "How many of each?"

"I need forty-five for tonight and then split the others up so I get an equal amount of each. They are for the restaurant. We will give them away until they are gone."

"I'm glad you had such success with the contest. I wish the police would have a little luck catching the killer we have wandering around here. I believe

I'm more nervous now that he isn't shooting people. Waiting for something to happen is stressful.

"I bet he finds away around the guards on the roof before long."

"Janice, that's no way to think. I bet the police are all over it."

"Arizona, of course you think that, your boyfriend is the chief of police."

I grinned at her. "Even if he wasn't, I'd have utter confidence he will catch the perp." A look at the clock on the wall told me the afternoon had flown past.

She handed me the copies. "Thanks so much for doing this, Janice. I think we will all be safe as long as the guards stay on the roofs."

CHAPTER 66

My phone rang. Keith. "Hi, how's it going?"

He said matter of factly, "We found Larry Eastburn's car."

"Really? That brings you a step closer. Where is it?"

Keith hesitated. "It's in our impound lot. It's been there since two days after Jackson Ramp was killed. According to Amanda, she found it near the Court House in a tow-away-zone. She left it there all day to see if someone was in court and just parked in the wrong place. She got busy and didn't go back. The next day, it was still parked there, so she had it towed to our lot.

"Of course no one has tried to claim it. I'm not sure what it means. Either he is still in town or found another way to leave. I have officers checking every place he could be staying within twenty-miles."

"What did you do with my Aunt Sandy?"

"She is home now. One of the auxiliary officers will be at your party tonight. Sandra remembered Larry Eastburn vividly. Seems he intimidated her all those years ago and even offered her money to say she didn't see Junior swing the car. She wouldn't do it.

"I called in both of his surviving sons. They are cooperative. They both said pretty much the same thing. Their dad went off the deep end when Junior died. They are both younger and said life as they knew it ended that day.

"Their mother said if they didn't leave Moonstone Lake, she would divorce him. Both boys said it didn't change much. He's a man obsessed.

"I won't be by tonight. It is slow going looking for a man you know is armed and a killer. If we find him, I will let you know."

"How's your leg?"

"Much better, thanks for taking me to the hospital this morning. Where are you looking for Eastburn?"

"We have an APB out all over the state. Since he killed everyone we believe he set out to kill, except for Sandra, we think he is close. The Highway Patrol has troopers going door to door in town in case someone he knew in his past has put him up. The sheriff has deputies checking all the hotels, motels and B&Bs to see if they can find him.

"His oldest boy sent us a photo. We have circulated it to every news outlet, TV station and newspaper around. We even passed them out to all of the stores in town in case he drops by one of them.

"We'll find him. You have put a lot of work into this contest. Eat dinner and relax. There will be an officer with Sandy all night. The only way he can get to her is to come inside. If he does that, we'll have him."

"Good luck and be careful. I've got to go," I said.

Chapter 67

Keith had sent a Highway Patrol Trooper to guard the front door and another to stand watch at the back. The event was semi-formal and by invitation only, so letting the wrong person in might have proved difficult.

We gave one gift away during each course. Aunt Sandy was in charge of it. She had everyone's name in a large fishbowl in front of the room. For the appetizer round, she drew the name and gave a set of six ramekins.

For the soup round, she gave away a solid white soup tureen. The salad gift comprised of one large wooden salad bowl, four small ones and a wooden fork and spoon to round out the set.

For the main dish drawing, she drew a name and presented the winner with a set of three Corning Ware baking pans, and last but not least, the dessert winner took home an oven proof skillet and lid.

The party ended a little after ten. Although everyone had fun, I believe everyone wanted to go home.

Keith called around eleven and said they had no luck finding the suspect. They narrowed their leads down to two possible hiding places, either a boat somewhere near or around the lake or he had retreated to the woods.

The good news, no more killings since Arlene Mann.

Chapter 68

The smell of popcorn filled my apartment. Keith sat on the couch holding a beer. Nutmeg laid by his feet, and I sat next to him. The most normal night we'd had since Jackson Ramp died.

Liz and Randy were on their way over. The movie we rented, The Quiet Place, was in the DVD. We all needed a mental health night.

We watched the movie, laughed and kidded like we did before the festival and all of the mayhem started. Keith, Randy and Liz's phones all began to ring at the same time. They glanced at one another. "Dispatch," Keith said.

"Same here," Randy added.

Liz joined in. "Emergency tip line."

Then silence while the three of them moved apart and listened to the people on the other end of their phones. I watched their faces. Liz hung up first. "Someone reported shots fired at the Duncan Marina. My editor wants me to check it out."

Keith and Randy hung up simultaneously. Keith passed on the contents of the call. "A 911 call came in. Matt Conner said his wife left him a note saying she was going to take their boat to the Crab Shack to meet her friends and she would be back before dark.

"He got home about eight, the house was dark and the boat was in its slip. He called the restaurant and Sharon never made it. He said the boat looks like a person has been living on it. Pizza boxes, fast food bags, beer bottles and more trash, no Sharon."

The three of them headed for their coats, so I did, too. I nodded toward Nutmeg. "We're going, too."

Liz was out the door. "I need my camera and tablet. Meet you downstairs."

The Conners were a couple in their late sixties. Matt retired as the high school football coach and Sharon as an English teacher. They lived in a lovely two-story home on the east end of the lake. Their home had its own dock. They were both known for using the boat to go back and forth to different destinations on the lake. Their Sea Ray had a closed cabin so winter didn't stop them unless we accumulated enough ice to damage the hull.

Matt paced up and down the dock from his back door to the boat and back again. I watched him intently. I'd say he didn't know what else to do.

Randy and Keith boarded the boat and disappeared below deck. Liz took numerous photos of the exterior of the vessel, and I nosed around the outside looking for, well, I didn't know what for sure.

Randy came back to the dock holding a high-powered rifle with an ink pen through the trigger guard to keep from leaving fingerprints. He no sooner set foot on the dock than I saw flashing lights. Jess Morgan had arrived with two men from his CSI team.

Jess laid out a large evidence bag and unzipped it. Randy carefully laid the gun on it. He looked toward Liz and me. "It's a .243. From the looks of the place, I'd say someone has been staying here for several days. You would have thought someone would have seen him coming or going."

Jess quietly dusted the gun for prints. Whoever it belonged to didn't try to wipe it clean. As Jesse finished with his task he said, in a delayed response, "My wife and I took our boy to the festival the other night. I passed right by people and didn't see them until they spoke. There is too much hustle and bustle to notice anything out of the ordinary."

Keith called Matt Conner to the boat and they both went below. Thirty minutes or so later they reemerged. Matt had tears in his eyes and Keith looked like he'd lost his best friend. "No sign of Sharon," he said to no one in particular.

The Coast Guard had four small boats in the water and powerful lights skimming the surface. The longer we were there, the more inconsolable Matt Conner became.

Keith called for an ambulance to administer to him.

The search went on for hours. The Coast Guard called off the search until morning. Jess and his CSI team left some hours later. To the distress of Mr. Conner, Keith sent two officers into the house as a precaution.

They found nothing. Keith spoke to Matt for a long minute, patted him on the shoulder and said they would continue the search at first light.

Keith went to the station. Liz and I rode home with the Highway Patrol Trooper who would take over from the one who'd been watching Aunt Sandy's apartment.

I didn't take the time to look at my phone for the time, but I knew the sun would rise soon.

I showered, fed Nutmeg and fell exhausted on my bed.

Since the spirit of Mother visited me— which had only been nine days ago— seemed like a distant memory, I'd never had time to put the entire story of my life in its proper place.

Did it have a proper place?

I took out the picture Emma gave me and sat it on my bedside table so when I turned on my right side, I could see it. At fifteen, when she left her parents' home, she looked much older. Her chiseled jaw, deep set green eyes and olive skin gave a unique look to her face. The red hair didn't fit. I could tell from the picture, and again from the night we met, it had never been dyed.

Never having been a mother, I didn't know for sure how she survived losing me, but I could somewhat understand why.

Nutmeg was only a dog, and I couldn't begin to compare the loss of her to the loss of a child. But I knew if she disappeared without a trace, I would look for and miss her forever.

I'd never thought about how it would be to be a mother. I liked my life. For the two years I'd been dating Keith, marriage never entered my mind.

It all boiled down to, no matter what happened to me as a child, I'd had a wonderful life, raised by Mom who risked everything to steal me from a home in another state and hide my identity for her friend.

Aunt Sandy, who never questioned where I came from, took me into her heart and eventually became my best friend.

And there was Lewis, who cooked me dinner every evening, sat with me in the café kitchen while I did my homework and brought me chicken noodle soup when I had a fever.

I reached over and touched the picture of Angela Reed Sanders' face and then the pendant I wore around my neck.

How I wished I could relay the story of the spirit of my mother, but I couldn't. I thought in time I might be able to, but now, thinking about it again, I realized it would lose its magic if I ever put it in words to another human.

I doubt if anyone would believe me. They would dismiss it as a dream.

CHAPTER 69

With all of the activity from the festival, the sniper, and the cooking contest, I hadn't closed the restaurant for weeks. It was time I gave Aunt Sandy and Benny a break and let them leave early.

I looked around my apartment. Little by little it got more cluttered with clothes and papers. There for a while, I did a decent job. But I did have to admit, when it came to cleaning, my standards were low.

My apartment consisted of two bedrooms, two baths, a kitchen, living room and laundry room with a washer and dryer. I had more than enough room to have a place for every item I owned. Mom said it was a flaw I had. She said I was allergic to cleaning.

Liz Austin moved into the downstairs apartment across from Mother's after the murder of her ex-husband. The people involved trashed her apartment. She'd been an artist all of her life. The creeps who tore up her things poured paint on a life time's worth of paintings.

She used her extra bedroom as an art studio, although she did have a twin bed in there in case she had company.

Mom used her extra room as a guest room/office. Although since her friends began their toy business, boxes of toys sat on the bed, the dresser, and every other flat surface in there. If she did have company spend the night, the only place to put them would be the couch.

Aunt Sandy lived upstairs across from me. We all had the same layout. Mine was a mirror image of Sandy's and the same with Mom and Liz downstairs.

I, on the other hand, slept in one bedroom until it got too messy then moved to the other one. When they were both equal, I cleaned both up and let it happen again.

Mom and Aunt Sandy never visited me. Mom didn't want to manage the stairs and Sandy didn't like the clutter.

She used her spare room as a library. She had more books than our local one. I believe she missed her calling. She should have been a librarian or a literature teacher. However, same as me, she was born into the Summers family where the relatives took it for granted you would want to work in the food services industry.

The rivalry between my mother's side of the family and her sister's family was legendary.

Five generations ago, my great, great, great,

great, great grandmother opened Moonstone Lake Café. It has never changed locations and is the oldest continuously owned family restaurant in the state and only one of less than a dozen in the country.

Before Granny died, she made out an iron clad will. It stated the youngest daughter in the next generation would inherit the business and her mother would retire on her seventieth birthday.

Until Mom, all of the women in the family were direct descendants of hers. Her sister and her brother both had all boys. A codicil stated if there were no girls in either family the café would be turned over to the youngest boy in the family.

It would have been my cousin Benjamin had Mother not come to Arizona, stole me and adopted me.

Lawsuit after lawsuit failed to turn the restaurant over to the men. The argument went, since Mother didn't have children of her own, it wasn't right for an adopted child to inherit the enterprise.

Each time they filed against my mother, a judge ruled against them. This went on for years until my aunt Ethyl died and her brother ran out of money to pursue losing legal fights.

With all of this going on from the time Emma adopted me to the time my mother told me about stealing me from an orphanage and why, I believed she wanted me only so she wouldn't lose the business.

I'd given it a lot of thought over the past weeks. Mom had risked prosecution, as did all of those who had to have helped her get me an identity and a birth certificate and who knows what else to protect me from my father's family. For all those years, none of them ever leaked a word about the circumstances of my arrival in Moonstone Lake.

I gave my mom grief several times a year, telling her she only adopted me to keep the restaurant. In reality, she saved me from no telling what kind of life. Her loyalty to me and her friend was truly amazing.

She kept all of the details bottled up inside her and didn't even tell Aunt Sandy so as to protect me. I was blessed, had been blessed for my entire life and didn't realize it.

My thoughts were interrupted by the phone. "Hi, I'm downstairs. Randy and Amanda and I decided to grab some lunch before Amanda goes to the airport in Stanfield."

"Why is she going to the airport?"

"Do you have a minute to join us? We are at your booth waiting for our food."

"I'll be right down."

CHAPTER 70

"Come on, Nutmeg, our morning off is over. Let's go downstairs."

A few minutes later I scooted onto the booth's bench next to Keith. "What did I miss?" I asked.

"Ah, where to begin?" Keith said. "I received a phone call from Eastburn's youngest son, Everett. He and his older brother, Ed, met at their father's house and what they found shocked them.

"Every newspaper account of their brother's death was out on the dining room table along with pictures of people they couldn't identify. They had bullseyes drawn on their faces. They packed it up and they are flying down here with it.

"Their plane comes in at 3:30. We are hoping it will give us some insight as to where he might be and what he's done with Sharon Conner." Alice brought their lunch and I sat with them while they ate. "The Coast Guard assures us she is not in the lake. And the Highway Patrol has had cadaver dogs out all day and they found nothing.

"My guess is he doesn't want to let her go because he doesn't think we know who he is. I think he has her stashed somewhere. The boys are going to be very vocal and make sure they are seen everywhere. We hope it will convince him we do know who he is. He'd no longer have a reason to hold Mrs. Conner."

I put both my elbows on the table and rested my chin on the heels of my hands. "I wish I didn't have to close tonight. All of this will be over and you'll have all the information you need before I am done here."

Amanda's phone buzzed. She took it out to read a text. "Arizona, you might not miss anything. Their flight was delayed in Denver. They won't be in until after ten. By the time I get back here with them, and get them checked in at Granny's, it will be too late to ask them to begin a long interrogation and explanation of their father and his habits and thoughts about the long ago death of his son."

Aunt Sandy and I closed together with the ever-present guard Keith insisted she have with her at all times. "Want to have a glass of wine when we finish here?" she asked.

"Sure, it's just what we need. I don't think we have sat down and relaxed for weeks. I had Randy, Liz and Keith over the other night to watch a movie. We got interrupted by a 911 call about Sharon Conner. It's always something since this madman decided to take revenge on an accident from twenty years ago."

"Let's make a deal," she said. "No talking about murder, death or Larry Eastburn. I haven't been anywhere but the café, home and back to the café. I miss the bookstore and Hugga-Mugga. This needs to be over."

CHAPTER 71

I set my morning alarm for five. I could shower, dress, walk Nutmeg, check on the restaurant and be at the police station by eight o'clock in time for the interview with Everett and Edward Eastburn.

The meeting took place in the conference room. The Eastburn brothers were tall, well-built and good-looking. Everett stood about six-feet three. He wore his short-cropped hair in a military style and had warm and friendly smokey green eyes. I liked him instantly.

The younger man, Edward, had lighter hair and a longer hairstyle and penetrating blue eyes. He seemed more reserved. He carried the shoe box he had with him as if it were a bomb about to explode. He set it gently on the table and pushed it toward Keith.

Keith put both hands on the box but didn't open

it until he said, "I want to thank you for calling us. We have lost several members of our community to a man we believe is your father. Let me introduce the people who are here with me."

He started on his left. "This is Trooper Matt Johnson from the Highway Patrol, next is Deputy James Neighbor from the Catoosa County Sheriff's office, and you know Officer Amanda Watts. Next to her is Officer Randy Malone and Arizona Summers who often consults with us on murder cases."

Everette looked toward the back of the room. "Who is the lady in the back?"

"I'm sorry," Keith smiled. "That is Nutmeg. She is Arizona's dog. Shall we get started?" He stood and walked to the front of the room where he pulled down a bulletin board. It took up three-fourths of the wall. He turned back and opened the box.

It contained newspaper articles, pictures and hand-written notes the men said were written in their father's writing.

Two hours later, the entire board held the last twenty years of Larry Eastburn's life.

In the center were newspaper accounts of Larry, Jr.'s death. Next to them were the entire transcripts of the trials of Walter (Bud) Watkins, our mayor and a picture of all of the victims.

We found a written list of people with a line through each of them except Sandra Jackson.

One newspaper story from a paper in Northern Wisconsin told of the death of Bud Williams. Tragically, the story recounted. Bud had been released from prison after he served seven years of a ten-year sentence. He was told to stay away from carnivals and not to accept any job that had anything to do with the carnival world.

The next story talked about how Bud died when a hit and run driver struck him as he walked across the roadway, only three weeks after his release.

There was a note on the article, Edward said his father wrote it. It said, *one down.*

Keith called Mary from the front desk. "Can you check this out and let me know if it is true? If so, please pull up the details."

"What did your mother think about your father's inability to view your brother's death as an accident?" Keith asked.

Everette answered. "It was a point of contention between them. I heard Mom tell him more than once that she couldn't put Larry to rest because of our dad's anger.

"It didn't matter what she said, he became obsessed, especially with those who testified that Larry stood in the seat and tried to rock the car over the top of the rail.

"Truth is, the entire football team rode the Ferris Wheel that night. Each and every one of them tried to force the cars over the top. It was a contest they were having. It just so happened Larry was the only one of his friends on that particular ride and the pins holding the seat to the framework sheared when he was on the ride."

Edward added, "It never came up how many boys might have tried to swing the car before Larry's ride. Dad would not hear anything about the football team. He had blinders on. In his mind,

Larry never did anything wrong. He was Dad's golden boy.

"He went after Bud Williams the night it happened. He beat him so badly Williams had to go to the hospital. If the police hadn't stopped Dad, I think he would have killed him there and then."

One more thing, Everett added, "There is no doubt in my mind, somehow Dad killed Bud Williams after he was released from jail. Dad traveled back then. It would have been nothing for him to go to Wisconsin and kill the man."

Edward's face turned crimson. "Dad is not a violent man. No one could have asked for a better dad. After Larry died, he became overly protective, but Everett and I understood. I got hit in the head with a line drive in a baseball game in high school. His reaction was to go after the boy who hit the ball. Again, his rage became uncontrollable at an unforeseen accident."

A knock on the door stopped our conversation. "A woman swears she saw Mr. Eastburn in the Discount Grocery store. One of the customers tried to follow him but Eastburn turned a corner, waited for the man, stepped out of the shadows and hit the customer so hard he fell back and hit his head on the sidewalk."

Keith looked at both sons. "My goal is to arrest your father without harming him. I want you to know if he gets hurt, it will be because it was unavoidable. Also, we haven't told you, but he lived on a boat for about a week. When the owner came out to use it, she disappeared, and we haven't been able to find her.

"She had nothing to do with your brother's accident, or any trial, and I doubt she knew who your father was until she met him on the boat."

"So, what's your plan?" Edward asked.

CHAPTER 72

Keith's plan included putting the Eastburn men on TV, the radio and in the Moonstone Reflection.

They looked at one another. "We can do that," said Edward. Everett shook his head *yes* in agreement.

We broke for lunch and planned to meet in an hour. Keith thought the Eastburns needed a break.

I wondered if they had any qualms about pleading with their dad on the media. It would go wide. All three TV networks from the Stanfield stations, our closest outlets, were scheduled to arrive later in the afternoon.

Liz would be at the interview with a photographer and four of Stanfield's radio stations, plus PBS and our local news station would all send someone to cover the event. I thought he would be most likely to hear it on our local station because it ran twenty-four/seven during the festival. They told of vendor sales, where the food trucks were located, and every hour on the hour the host told the up-to-the-minute news of the happenings of Moonstone Lake.

Normally the news consisted of who died, their funeral arrangements, who was in the hospital, getting married, divorced and who had company from out of town.

Keith still didn't want any of us to walk around alone. During the day there were four roof guards for the entire town. At night there were nine.

None of us thought Eastburn would try to kill anyone from a long distance. His rifle lay in the evidence room at the police station under lock and key. His sons said their dad had three pistols and a 22 rifle, all at his home in Oklahoma.

My concern fell on Aunt Sandy. After seeing the files he kept all these years, I knew he would not want to give up until he killed her.

Keith and the others must have believed the same because Aunt Sandy now had a guard at the front door of the café, one at the back, one inside the apartment building outside her door and another at the first table in the dining room.

We all went our separate ways at lunch time. The Eastburns went to Granny's to shower and then to get a bite to eat at the Moonstone Café.

Keith stayed at the station to help set up a space for the interviews. Amanda and Randy went to grab a taco, and I took Nutmeg for a walk against the better judgement of all parties concerned.

CHAPTER 73

The pleas for Larry Eastburn, Sr, from his sons was gut wrenching. "Dad," Edward began, "you have gone through this town and ruined lives. It didn't bring Larry back. Nothing will bring him back. Please surrender to the police. They will guarantee your safety. Please, don't hurt anyone else. This is not the man I know and love. The man who spent hours on his knees in the backyard catching for me so I could become a pitcher.

"This is not the man who acted out the characters in the books you read us when we were kids. Please don't destroy all those memories. If you think about it, you know Larry would not approve of your actions. Please, Dad, please."

"Dad," Everett took over. "Please release Sharon Conner. That's the name of the woman you kidnapped from her boat. She has done nothing and had no part in Larry's accident. She didn't even know about it until you began killing her friends and neighbors.

"Edward and I will be in town until you turn yourself in. I beg you, don't hurt anyone else. As Everette said, 'Nothing will bring Larry back or ease the torture you have gone through in your mind all these years.' We know you have one more person on your list. Don't go near her, she only did what you would have done were the situation reversed. We love you, Dad. We always have. We miss Larry, too. He was our big brother, we looked up to him. Please show yourself and let the police take you into custody and put an end to this horror."

For the next four days, the town held its breath. Between the news outlets, the public service announcement the Eastburn brothers made played over two hundred times.

Hope about finding Sharon Conner alive waned as time passed.

The people who participated in the festival, the vendors and customers from out of town didn't seem too concerned about the killer we had running loose. Once they found out why he killed the victims they acted like nothing was wrong.

The rest of us were on pins and needles. Aunt Sandy became depressed. She hadn't been out on her own for weeks. The constant fear a bullet would come out of nowhere and take her life took her joy.

Nutmeg and I tried to go back to normal with a morning run and an evening run. We did begin later in the morning and earlier in the evening.

We were on our way to the north side of town to

load up on junk food when we passed a car that piqued Nutmeg's interest. She began to run around and around it and would not stop or go any farther.

I called 911. "There is a red Nissan Altima parked in the middle of the block on Church Street. Nutmeg will not leave the area. Would you please send someone? The car is in front of the old record store building."

Maybe in other cities, if a person called in and said their dog thought something was amiss, they might blow it off. In Moonstone Lake, no one doubted Nutmeg's ability to pick out a problem. And more times than not, solve it. I sat on the curb and waited.

Nutmeg stopped running and sat behind the car, in front of the trunk, and whined.

A cold chill went through me as I began to imagine what might be in there.

Keith showed up first, sirens blaring and lights flashing. Next, Randy pulled up in the other direction. He looked in the windows and checked the doors. Randy handed him a slim-jim, a long flat piece of metal Keith ran down beside the front door window. A few seconds later, he had the door unlocked.

He opened the door and looked inside. In the glove compartment, he found a registration card. Jacob Morris, Fort Wayne, Indiana. I knew him to be the owner of the funnel cake food truck.

"Randy, go down to Jacob's food truck and ask him for the keys to this car. Tell him he is not in trouble. If he feels the need to come back with you, so be it. If he doesn't know anything might be wrong with the car, he won't feel the need to come."

Ten minutes later, Randy came back with a set of keys and permission to open the trunk.

Meanwhile, Nutmeg hadn't moved. She sat on guard in front of the trunk. Keith knelt on one knee and looked straight into the dog's eyes. "I need for you to move over and let me see what you found. You're a good girl but you can't do this on your own. Can you move for me?"

Nutmeg turned and trotted over to me about ten feet away and sat by my foot. Keith opened the lid and said with alarm in his voice, "Randy, get an ambulance here, now. It's Sharon Conner."

He put his finger to her neck. "She has a pulse, but it is weak. We need to get her out of this confined area so she can get some air.

"Arizona, can you get me an emergency blanket from the back of my cruiser and spread it out on the sidewalk so we can lay her on it."

Within a minute, Randy and Keith had Sharon out of the trunk and on the ground. She didn't move, but I saw her chest lightly go up and down. Keith put his ear next to her mouth. "She is breathing. She's cold, malnourished, and in shock. I wish they would get here."

It was then we heard the sirens. EMT's showed up and right behind them Jess Morgan rolled up and behind him, some of his crew in a different car.

No one made a sound. I noticed I'd been holding my breath. One of the paramedics had the hospital on the phone. Another started an IV and put an oxygen tube over her head and into her nose. She took a breath we could all see.

The ambulance crew worked on her for another ten minutes. I heard Jimmy Phillips tell the hospital, "I don't see any noticeable injuries. Is it okay to transport her? Her pulse is 53, respiration's 9 and temperature 95.4."

They left immediately.

"Randy, call Mr. Conner. Tell him we found his wife, tell him she is alive and on her way to the hospital. Don't tell him anything else until the ER doctor has a chance to look her over."

Keith looked at Nutmeg who had sat quietly next to me for the entire ordeal. He came over to her. He reached down to shake her hand. "You are a marvel, Nutmeg. Thank you."

Nutmeg got up, walked around Keith twice and licked his face, barked once and came back to sit by my foot.

CHAPTER 74

Nutmeg and I rode over to the hospital with Keith. Sharon Conner lay in an emergency cubicle with her husband near her side. She opened her eyes, looked around and closed them again.

She spoke in a weak voice but never opened her eyes again. "The man said his name was Larry Eastburn. He let me know right away he was the sniper. He asked me if I knew the story of his son's murder." She stopped. Her voice had little strength to it. I thought she fell asleep. After a long moment, she continued. "He asked me if I thought he was wrong to kill those people. I told him it wasn't up to me to judge. He took me to the car you found me in. I knew I would die in that trunk. The nights were so cold, and in the daytime the sun beat down on the trunk lid. It got so hot I couldn't catch my breath.

"I was aware when someone walked by, but I

didn't have the strength to kick or knock or call out. Have you caught him?"

"Shhh…" her husband said, "rest now. You're safe."

Keith and I walked out into the hall. Nutmeg lay immediately outside the Emergency Room door. She wagged her tail when I looked her way. "I need to go home. Nutmeg hasn't had her dinner, and I doubt Eastburn will show his face tonight."

"I'll take you. Let me post a guard outside Mrs. Conner's room and I'll be ready."

"We can walk," I said.

Keith put one hand on each of my shoulders and brought me close to him. His penetrating black eyes looked into mine. "No, you can't," he said.

When I arrived at my apartment building, a trooper opened the downstairs door for me. I walked up the stairs and a sheriff's deputy insisted he go into my apartment before I did to make sure it was safe.

The thought occurred to me that when this ordeal ended, I would have every lock and pass code changed. It seemed every state trooper, sheriff's deputy and police officer could walk in any time they wanted. I hoped if they had the codes written down, they were careful with them.

I doubted Keith would call if nothing new happened. I'd talked to him or overheard all the new developments.

Liz called. "Hi, thought I'd check in. All these police make me paranoid. They insisted on checking my apartment before I could come in."

I sat on the couch and patted the space next to

me for Nutmeg to join me. "I can only imagine what my Aunt Sandy goes through. I guess it is a better-safe-than-sorry situation."

"The big interview with Larry Eastburn's sons comes out tomorrow. I have already heard it several times on the local station. They play it every hour on the hour, hoping he is somewhere where he hears it," she said. "If we get no feedback, no tips on the tip line or no one calls in to say they spotted him, David Dorman said he will offer a reward for information on the behalf of the victims."

I stopped rubbing Nutmeg and took a sip of the wine I poured earlier. "How much will the reward be, did he say?"

"Fifty thousand dollars."

"Used cars must be profitable," I said, half joking."

"He comes from money. He is always the first to give and gives the most. I like him. He pays for funerals for people who don't have the money, gives cars away. Just a top-of-the-line guy."

"What do you think happens next?"

"Well, I came from the newsroom about an hour ago. Keith dropped by and spoke to Mr. Sparks about leaving the front page open so they could announce the reward if the interviews tonight did no good. I think they plan another public plea for information tomorrow afternoon.

"Gotta go. Randy is on his way in. I haven't seen him, except from a distance since the movie at your place. Catch ya later. Stay safe." She hung up before I had a chance to say another word.

270

CHAPTER 75

I heard a commotion outside. The café had been packed a moment ago, now all the diners were scrambling to get outside.

Nutmeg must have gone with the crowd because when I got to the front where she slept, it was empty.

Even Aunt Sandy and her guards were on their way to the sidewalk. I couldn't get through the mob. I went back through the door, walked to the back and went out.

Lewis followed me. "I can't imagine what it is," he said.

As I hurried through The Gray Goose's parking lot and out front, I ended up a good two blocks down the street from the restaurant.

Both sides of the street were lined with rubberneckers. At one end stood Randy, Amanda, two troopers, Keith and the Eastburn brothers. Nutmeg lay about halfway between the authorities and a man who walked slowly toward them.

I knew it had to be Larry Eastburn, Senior. He held a pistol in his right hand and a knife in his left. No doubt in my mind. He hadn't come to give himself up. He came to fight. I prayed Aunt Sandy was nowhere in his line of sight.

Keith took two steps forward so he stood alone. It looked like movies I'd seen where the lawman and the bad guy had a shootout in the middle of the street. "Stop where you are and lay your weapons on the pavement."

Eastburn took a step forward. Keith took a step forward. "Mr. Eastburn, this does not have to end badly. Enough people have suffered in this ordeal. This is the last time I am going to tell you. Put the gun and knife down and get on your knees with your hands behind your head."

The man put his head back and laughed. "It's too late for this to turn out any way but badly.

"If you want me to stop, you'll have to shoot me. Save the state the expense of a trial and put me out of my misery. I'm not sorry for killing those people. They took my boy away from me."

Keith pointed behind him. "What about the men standing behind the police there? They're your boys and I've talked to them. They are good decent men. Put the gun down and let's not carry this on any further."

Eastburn's face turned red with rage. "Don't talk about my boys. You know nothing. The stories the police and witnesses told are not the truth. Everyone lied to save this town and this stupid light show. It all meant more to you people than my boy."

Out of the corner of my eye, I saw Nutmeg on the move. She crawled an inch at a time toward the killer. I held my breath. Eastburn had stopped in the street, about twenty paces from Keith.

Nutmeg had cleared half the distance between where she lay before and where the man stood. My heart pounded in my head. If one person said a word of warning to Eastburn, or if he looked down and saw my dog, I knew he would kill her.

Before I could take another breath, Nutmeg sprang forward, leaped into the air and came down with a shocked Larry Eastburn's hand, which held the gun, in her teeth.

He screamed and tried to shake her loose. It took him a few seconds to realize what happened, and he whirled the knife toward Nutmeg's head.

Keith yelled, "No," at the same time he tackled the man and threw him to the ground. Randy came to his aide within a few seconds. The man lay in the middle of the street, writhing in pain. Nutmeg had never let go of his hand. The gun had fallen to the ground thirty seconds earlier, still, Nutmeg shook her head back and forth with her mouth tightly closed.

"Nutmeg, you can let go. Nutmeg," Keith yelled at her. She stopped thrashing, but she didn't release the man's hand. "Arizona, if you can hear me, please call off your dog. Would someone please get Arizona Summers?"

When I reached the scene, I walked to Nutmeg's side and whispered in her ear. "Nutmeg. You did a fine job. Let go and let Keith do his." She held on a few more seconds and let go. The entire place exploded with people chanting, "Nutmeg, Nutmeg, Nutmeg." The words became louder and more rhythmic. It went on for a good five minutes.

I heard a siren and two EMT's were at Eastburn's side tending to his hand. Keith and Randy had him pinned to the ground. The Troopers, and his sons stood close. They couldn't handcuff him because of his injury.

Randy reached behind him and put a cuff on the sniper's uninjured hand. He put the other one on a wrought iron bench.

The ordeal had ended.

On New Year's Day, the town had the usual end of the Moonstone Lake Festival of Lights parade. The mayor had Nutmeg in a convertible in the front and announced her as Grand Marshall.

The event I most worried about happened. People took cell phone videos of my dog as she took down the killer. She made the national news.

Since I'd had the dog, and realized how special she was, I'd sheltered her from the limelight. Liz had wanted to write a story about Nutmeg and the wonderous things she'd done for the last two years, and I'd always said no.

Now, with the cell phone videos and Nutmeg and me being invited to New York to the Today Show, I had to allow it.

I only hoped Nutmeg stayed the same humble companion she'd always been to me.

CHAPTER 76

Nutmeg's picture and the way she attacked the sniper monopolized the front page of the Moonstone Reflection. The Stanfield paper and the St. Louis Star all ran similar stories.

The phone at the restaurant began to ring constantly. It wasn't for reservations. The calls came from all over the nation. People wanted Nutmeg's help to find missing persons, killers and to ask if Nutmeg and I would come on their talk show.

I said *no* to all of them, including the Today Show.

Keith and I were relaxing in my living room watching reruns of Seinfeld. I said, "Aren't you glad to have this over with?"

"And I don't even have to house him at the jail. When he confessed to Sharon Conners about killing

Bud Williams, it became a case for the FBI.

"I have one more arrest to make before the crafters begin to go home."

"Really?" I said. "Who's that?"

"Sadie Maxwell, well Renee Dover. I hate to do it, but the law is the law. You can't get a social security number, credit cards and checking accounts of a dead person. Even when someone goes into witness protection, their identity isn't from a dead person.

"Would you like to go along? The FBI is going to meet me there in the morning."

"No, I think I'll pass. The lady made a horrible mistake that killed her entire family. Since then there is no indication she ever broke another law. Can't you let her go?"

"Ary, I thought about it, but I can't. Sorry. Maybe the Feds will see it your way, but I need to do my job."

"I understand. Can we not talk about killers and criminals anymore tonight?"

Keith scooted over close to me and put his arm on the back of the couch. "We are alone, everything is quiet, the murders are solved. What do you want to talk about?" he asked, as he leaned over to kiss me.

THE END

ABOUT THE AUTHOR

Susan Keene has been writing full time for the past ten years. She loves to write mysteries readers can't solve. Her Arizona Summers Mystery series reached #1 on Kindle.

The Kate Nash Series is popular and a fourth book in each series will hit the shelves this year.

She does her best to write each book as a stand-alone.

Susan won her first literary award at age 16.

She lives on a farm in the Missouri Ozarks.

Chili, the dog in the Kate Nash Series is patterned after her real dog and companion, Chili, who just turned 5.

Nutmeg, the dog in the Arizona Summers Mysteries, is a composite of several of the dogs on the farm. There are eight.

Her three grandchildren and her daughter and sister are a great joy. She loves vegetable gardening, walking around the farm with her metal detector and reading.

Winner, Appetizer Recipe

Prosciutto Cracker Appetizer

Prep time: 10 minutes   Cook time: 1 minute
  Total 11 minutes Serves 20
Ingredients:
7 oz whipped cream cheese
1 ½ tsp olive oil
1 tbsp minced garlic
3 oz sliced Prosciutto
40 crackers (I use Captain's Wafers or Ritz)
Salt and pepper to taste
Chopped parsley for topping.
Honey to drizzle on top
In a small bowl, mix together cream cheese, garlic, olive oil, salt and pepper. Set aside.

Cut prosciutto into small rectangles.

Spread a small amount of mixture onto each cracker.

Roll each prosciutto up and place on top of the crackers.

Drizzle a small amount of honey over each and sprinkle with parsley.

The award-winning soup

Cold Cucumber Soup

Ingredients:
2 large English cucumbers, cut in half and

remove seeds. Cut ½ cup finely chopped, chop the rest coarsely

1 ½ cups plain Greek yogurt
3 tbsp fresh lemon
1 small shallot, chopped
1 clove garlic
1/3 cup loosely packed dill
¼ cup loosely packed parsley leaves
2 tbsp loosely packed tarragon leaves
¼ cup olive oil
Fresh ground pepper and salt to taste
½ red onion, finely chopped

In a blender, combine the coarsely chopped cucumber with the yogurt, lemon juice, shallot, garlic, dill, parsley. Tarragon and the ¼ cup olive oil. Blend until smooth. Salt and pepper to taste. Cover and refrigerate for at least 8 hours (I leave it overnight)

Season the soup again before serving. Pour the soup into bowls. Garnish with finely diced cucumber, red onion and a little drizzle of olive oil and serve.

Winning salad

Cranberry, Apple, Bleu Cheese Salad

Ingredients:
4 cups mixed greens
1 apple, cubed
½ cup walnuts

½ cup dried cranberries
¼ cup bleu cheese
¼ cup sweet Vidalia onion dressing

Prepare 4 bowls with mixed greens
Top with apple, walnuts, cranberries, bleu cheese then drizzle with Vidalia dressing.

Winning main dish

Tuscan Chicken Mac and Cheese

2 large skinless, boneless, chicken breasts, pounded to 1 inch thickness (It is okay to substitute 4 boneless and skinless chicken thighs)
Salt and pepper
½ tsp paprika
½ tsp dried parsley
1 tbsp oil (olive or canola)
2 tbsp butter
1 small chopped yellow onion
5 cloves garlic finely chopped
9 oz jar of sun-dried tomato strips in oil. Put 2 tbsp aside, drain the rest
3 tbsp flour
2 1/3 cups chicken broth
3 cups milk or light cream of half and half
2 tbsp Italian seasoning
10 ounce package of uncooked elbow macaroni
3 cups baby spinach leaves
1 cup fresh grated Parmesan cheese
¾ cup mozzarella cheese, shredded
½ cup grated cheddar cheese

1. Season chicken with salt, pepper, paprika and 2 tsp of the oil. Heat the remaining oil in a large pot or pan over medium heat. Add chicken and sear on both sides until golden brown, and is cooked through and no longer pink in the middle. Transfer the chicken to a warm plate, tent with foil and set aside.
2. To the same pan add the butter and fry the onion and garlic until the onion becomes transparent, stirring occasionally. Pour in 1/3 cup of chicken broth and allow to simmer for 5 minutes, or until it begins to reduce.
3. Add sun dried tomatoes with the 2 tbsp of the oil you saved from the jar. Cook for about 2 minutes.
4. Stir the flour into the pot and allow to cook for a minute. Then add the broth, 2 ½ cups of milk, herbs, salt, pepper, and bring to a low simmer.
5. Add the dry macaroni and stir occasionally as it comes to a simmer. Reduce to medium heat, stir regularly while it cooks, about 9 minutes or until the sauce thickens and the macaroni is tender, but firm (al dente). Add spinach and stir until wilted.
6. Remove pot from heat and stir all cheeses in quickly. Salt and pepper to taste. (if the sauce is too thick add the rest of the milk.)
7. Slice the chicken into strips and stir into the pasta (stir in any juices from the chicken) Sprinkle with parsley and stir. Serve immediately.

Winning dessert

Triple-chocolate Cheesecake

Ingredients:
Crust layer
¼ cup butter
½ cup sugar
3 tbsp baking cocoa
½ tsp vanilla
1 large egg, room temperature
¼ cup all-purpose flour
1/8 tsp baking powder
1/8 tsp salt
2 – 8-ounce packages of cream cheese

Directions:
Preheat oven to 350. Line a 9x13 pan with foil, letting ends extend up the sides, grease the foil. In a microwave, melt butter in a large bowl. Stir in sugar, cocoa and vanilla, Add egg, blend well. Add flour, baking powder and salt; stir until combined (only until combined.) Spread as a thin layer in prepared pan. Bake until the top appears dry, about 6-8 minutes

Cheesecake layer
2-8 ounces cream cheese
½ cup sugar
¾ cup semisweet chocolate chips
2 large eggs, room temp, slightly beaten

Directions:
In a large bowl beat cream cheese, sugar, and

vanilla until smooth. Beat in the cooled chocolate chips, add beaten eggs; beat on low speed just enough to combine. Spread over brownie layer. Bake until filling is set, 25-30 minutes. Cool 10 minutes on a wire rack.

Ganache:
1 ½ cups semi-sweet chocolate chips
½ cup heavy whipping cream
1 tsp vanilla extract

Directions:
Place chocolate chips in a small bowl. In a sauce pan bring cream to a boil. Pour over chocolate, let stand 5 minutes. Stir with a whisk until smooth, stir in vanilla, cool slightly, stirring occasionally. Pour over cheesecake layer. Cool in pan on a wire rack 1 hour. Refrigerate at least 2 hours. Lifting with foil, remove brownies from pan. Cut into bars.